His throat constricted. "Obviously, this changes everything," he said tightly. "I'm not having sex with a virgin," he snapped.

She was shaking her head, the glossy spill of copper curls tumbling down over her shoulders, and he wondered if she had any idea how lovely she looked right then.

"I still don't understand," she whispered. "You want sex with me and I definitely want sex with you. A piece of paper says we're legally married—so what's the problem? Please explain it to me."

He chose his words carefully. "The fact that you haven't been intimate with anyone else is significant."

"How?"

He shrugged. "It suggests you still care for me and will read too much into it," he continued repressively. "And I really don't want that to happen."

Mia stared back, her heart slamming hard against her rib cage as she took in what he'd just said. "Of all the arrogant things you've ever said to me, Theo Aeton, and there have been plenty of those," she breathed, "that one really tops the lot."

Sharon Kendrick once won a national writing competition by describing her ideal date: being flown to an exotic island by a gorgeous and powerful man. Little did she realize that she'd just wandered into her dream job! Today she writes for Harlequin, and her books feature often stubborn but always to-die-for heroes and the women who bring them to their knees. She believes that the best books are those you never want to end. Just like life...

Books by Sharon Kendrick

Harlequin Presents

Cinderella's Christmas Secret
One Night Before the Royal Wedding
Secrets of Cinderella's Awakening
Confessions of His Christmas Housekeeper
Her Christmas Baby Confession

Jet-Set Billionaires

Penniless and Pregnant in Paradise

Passionately Ever After...

Stolen Nights with the King

Visit the Author Profile page
at Harlequin.com for more titles.

Sharon Kendrick

INNOCENT MAID FOR THE GREEK

HARLEQUIN®
PRESENTS™

Recycling programs for this product may not exist in your area.

ISBN-13: 978-1-335-73902-5

Innocent Maid for the Greek

Copyright © 2023 by Sharon Kendrick

For questions and comments about the quality of this book, please contact us at CustomerService@Harlequin.com.

Harlequin Enterprises ULC
22 Adelaide St. West, 41st Floor
Toronto, Ontario M5H 4E3, Canada
www.Harlequin.com

Printed in U.S.A.

INNOCENT MAID FOR THE GREEK

For my darling friend Professor Richard Shannon, aka Dick (though I only ever knew him as Blaine, a name we concocted on our first meeting on discovering we shared a birthday). We enjoyed many lunches over the years, meticulously spitting the bill (he did rather better out of it than I!). He tried to teach me historical facts, which I promptly forgot (though never the origin of the color magenta).

He is sorely missed but always, always remembered.

CHAPTER ONE

SHE'D ONLY RECENTLY SHOWERED, but already another bead of sweat was sliding down between Mia's breasts.

If only it weren't so unbearably *hot*.

Fanning her hand in front of her face, she peered out of the window. The sky was heavy. Thick grey clouds were tinged with a sickly sulphuric yellow and she could hear the ominous growl of thunder in the distance. Definitely not the sort of weather you associated with an English spring day.

Sometimes she thought about Greece. The scent of lemon blossom and pine. Golden sun and the sea and sky so blue. But she never thought about it for long because why would you do something which actively caused you heartache?

A sudden knock on the door made her jump because she wasn't expecting anyone and that was deliberate. She kept her tiny one-room home as a haven—sometimes it even felt like an escape. Her job was sociable enough, but outside work and her animal volunteering she kept herself to herself. She knew people thought she was a loner. A bit of a frump, even. Let them. She did what she did because that was how she coped—with her life, with the past, and with the memories which stubbornly refused to leave the edges of her mind.

The knock sounded again and although it was tempting to ignore it, her conscience wouldn't let her. It might be an emergency involving one of the other hotel staff and she—sensible and reliable Mia, in her newly promoted position—would know exactly how to deal with it.

But her smile froze as she pulled open the door and saw who was standing there, dominating every atom of the space which surrounded him just as he'd always done, his powerful frame making the institutional background of the staff corridor look even more unexciting than usual.

His expensive grey suit did nothing to disguise the strength of the muscular body which rippled beneath. His face was all hard, slashing lines and high cheekbones. His skin had the burnished hue of deep gold, while his eyes gleamed like polished jet. It was easy to understand why people used to say he resembled an ancient Greek god, because he did.

Her husband.

How strange it was to acknowledge those

words—because he was her husband in name only. Well, not even that—not any more—for she always used her maiden name. She wanted nothing of his.

Theodoros Aeton.

The man she had loved so badly, until he had betrayed her and smashed her heart into tiny little pieces.

Clutching the doorhandle, she felt a wave of dizziness wash over her. And she felt other things, too. Unwanted emotions which had started bubbling up inside her, like random ingredients dropped into a witch's cauldron. Hurt and anger and resentment. And desire, of course. Always desire. She wasn't naïve enough to deny *that*.

It was a face she hadn't seen in six years. Not since the evening of their wedding when her world had imploded. She'd been wearing a slippery white gown, which had done her abundant curves no favours—but she had bowed to her mother's superior knowledge about all things fashionable.

Mia remembered the frilly blue garter and the white silk stockings which had been digging uncomfortably into her thighs, but she hadn't cared about the discomfort. She had just been eager for the moment when Theo would slowly remove them with his teeth, as he had promised he would do in a throaty murmur just the night before. Along with all the other things he had promised, too. In retrospect, his words had been nothing but manipulative, but at the time she had lapped them up like a thirsty kitten—naïve and oh, so gullible.

She wanted to shut the door on him, but that would be the behaviour of someone cowardly and immature. And she wasn't either of these things. Not any more. She'd grown up. She was making her own way in the world, without any help or assistance from anyone. Certainly not from Theo Aeton.

Even so, she wished she weren't wearing an old pair of jeans and a T-shirt which could have done with an iron. She wished she were ten pounds lighter. She wished all kinds of things, but since none of them were likely to materialise in the next few minutes, it was better she got this over and done with. And wasn't the reality that she'd been expecting some kind of contact from Theo for a long time, even if she hadn't allowed herself to think about it? Some sort of closure. A request for a long-overdue divorce most probably, in order to allow him to move on. And if the thought of that produced a twist of pain then *more fool her.*

His name sprang from her lips, sounding unfamiliar, yet somehow shockingly familiar. 'Theo!'

'Mia,' he responded, his husky Greek accent sliding over the syllables, which had the unfortunate effect of making her think about his tongue.

She tried to pull her incoherent thoughts into some sort of order but that was a big ask, when she couldn't seem to dislodge the memory of that tongue inside her mouth and on her neck and... With a supreme effort, she pulled herself together. 'Well, well, well. This is a surprise,' she said brightly. 'I must say you were the last person I expected to see when I knocked off work earlier today.'

'But here I am,' he prompted softly.

'Yes, here you are,' she echoed, her heart pounding wildly.

She peered at him more closely and suddenly she could see the change in him. He looked different. Almost...dangerous. His ravishingly handsome features seemed to have been coated in a layer of dark ice, which had the effect of making him seem cool. Formidable. Even *cruel*...

'Aren't you going to invite me in?' His voice was mocking. 'Or are you so blown away by seeing me again that you can't think straight?'

Irritated by his totally accurate assessment of her mood, Mia glared before opening the door a little wider, reluctance written in her every gesture. 'That's not how I would have described it, Theo, but since you've come all this way, I suppose you'd better come in.'

But quickly, she moved as far away as she could, not wanting to be close to him.

And you're a liar. You want to be close to him. You want him to pull you against that hard body and kiss all the breath out of your lungs. You want to remember how it feels to be in his arms. To remember how he made you feel as if *this* was the reason you were put here on this earth.

Stop it, she urged herself fiercely as she regarded him with a veneer of polite curiosity. 'Why didn't you give me some sort of warning you were coming, Theo? Why just turn up out of the blue?'

Shutting the door behind him, Theodoros Aeton took a moment before he answered, and not just because he was a man who always chose his words carefully. He was grappling with an uncharacteristic feeling of confusion. A sense of being taken off-guard because—infuriatingly—his reaction to her had taken him by surprise. He had expected to feel nothing when he saw her again. He had *wanted* to feel nothing—because a man who allowed himself to feel ran the risk of making himself vulnerable and hadn't he done that once before—with her?

His mouth twisted, because he *did* feel something. There was a residual anger, which mostly he kept buried away deep inside him, but there was bitterness, too. As bitter as the hyacinth bulbs which many of his native countrymen still ate, surprisingly for pleasure. Because this was the woman who had crushed his dreams. Whose words had reinforced what he'd always really known about himself and made him realise the only thing he could rely on was his innate streak of cynicism. It was that hard-wired cynicism he reached for now as he studied her, curious to see how much she had changed.

Physically, she didn't look so very different. Her shape was as voluptuous as ever, the curve of her hips and breasts still sending out a siren call to his senses. Small of stature, she was nothing like her lofty English supermodel mother—the thick chestnut hair was the only thing she seemed to have inherited from her. But her mother's hair had been sleek and coppery, and Mia's was a chaotic head of curls, currently scrunched up on top of her head with damp tendrils dangling down beside her flushed cheeks. Her proud features hinted at her Greek heritage—as did the jet-dark lashes which framed her slanting blue eyes and golden-olive skin. He didn't approve of her old jeans and crumpled T-shirt, but surely her lack of effort with her appearance implied she wasn't expecting someone else. Some faceless man he would have been forced to eject, by whatever means he considered appropriate. Theo's mouth hardened. He didn't know why that should give him a brief sense of pleasure, only that it did.

His gaze flickered around the cramped dimensions of the room. What *was* remarkably different were her circumstances. He glanced at the narrow bed, the utilitarian wardrobe and the small plywood locker which reminded him of a hospital.

Who would ever have imagined that Mia would end up living in a cramped room which overlooked a fire escape?

'I gave you no prior warning because I have always enjoyed the element of surprise,' he said, with a hard smile—and that was the truth. Hadn't he wondered what her instinctive reaction on seeing him again would be? Had he imagined her features might soften with signs of longing, or regret? But there had been nothing like that. Just wariness and a thinly veiled hostility which—bizarrely— pleased him. It reinforced his certainty of how ill-judged their liaison had been and the sooner he was properly free of her, the better.

'Well, you've achieved what you came for. I am *very* surprised,' she said, before adding curiously, 'Tell me, how did you find me?'

The cheap T-shirt clung to her breasts, and Theo felt his throat grow dry as his attention was unwillingly caught by their generous thrust. Breasts which were taunting him, reminding him that he'd placed her on that damned pedestal, insisting on telling her they wouldn't have full sex until she was his wife. He felt a stab of irritation as he recalled his foolish idealism. Why hadn't he just taken her to bed when he'd had the chance? All those times she had pressed against him and whimpered with raw desire—why had he insisted on doing the *decent thing*? 'The acquisition of information is never difficult for a man like me,' he informed her coolly. 'I paid for someone to discover your whereabouts.'

'Gosh! A private investigator, no less!' Her eyebrows shot up and disappeared into the mass of coppery curls. 'Am I supposed to be impressed?'

He shrugged. 'Why not? You're only human,' he mocked, but then reminded himself of the reason behind his visit and his voice softened. 'You need to come back to Greece, Mia. Your grandfather is sick.'

He saw her lips crumple. Saw the darkness which invaded those wide blue eyes, which were the colour of the Aegean on a bright spring day.

'How sick?' she whispered.

'What do you want me to say? That a man of almost eighty is bouncing around like a boxer? You might know something of his state of health if only you had bothered to keep in touch with him!'

'It isn't as simple as that,' she protested. 'You must know that, Theo. He cut me out of his life and said he never wanted to see me again! And every time I've tried to contact him, I have been rebuffed.'

'He was a proud man. Running away on your wedding night caused a scandal in the local neighbourhood. And you know how he felt about scandals.'

She bit her lip. 'I don't want to talk about that night.'

'Well, that's good because neither do I.' Theo

felt his jaw tighten and his muscles grow tense as he reminded himself he wasn't here because of the past, because that was over and done with. He was just doing a favour for an old man who didn't realise he needed one. A man to whom he owed everything. And if that meant having to see a woman whose memory he would rather have erased from his mind, then so be it. He could cope with that. With her. She was just somebody he used to know. 'You need to see him,' he reiterated. 'And soon.'

'Is he…dying?' The gaze she turned on him was so wretched that Theo could do nothing about the answering clench of his heart, and silently he cursed her for that, too.

'Yes, he is dying,' he said, his voice brittle. 'He is no longer the man he once was—with the heart of a lion and the body of an ox. Age has caught up on him, as it catches up on us all.' He saw the tell-tale glimmer of tears in her sea-blue eyes. 'You will be shocked when you see him again, Mia.'

She nodded. 'And did he…did he ask for me?'

There was a heartbeat of a pause before he answered, and Theo wondered how she would react if he told her the truth. But ultimately, she would thank him for his intervention because wasn't he giving her the chance to so something which had never been afforded to him? His mouth clenched. 'He needs to see you.' He glanced around the room. 'How quickly can you pack?'

His peremptory question reminded Mia how different their worlds were. They always had been—she just hadn't been able to see it at the time. Or maybe she hadn't wanted to. She had believed herself in love with him and, inevitably, that had distorted the way she'd viewed the world.

Since their split, she had stopped herself from stalking him on the Internet because that way lay madness, but she'd found a financial newspaper lying in one of the hotel bedrooms when she'd been cleaning it, and her attention had been captured by the brooding good looks of her estranged husband. Her eyes had quickly skimmed the text and she'd discovered how successful he was. A hedge-fund manager apparently—whatever *that* meant—though judging from his many assets she'd concluded that such a job was highly rewarded financially.

But even if she hadn't known how rich he was, she could tell just by looking at him. A sense of power radiated from him, in a way which was almost tangible. And hadn't he done it all off *her* back? She wondered if he felt a glimmer of shame for his actions, but she wasn't going to bring that up now. It would make it look as if she cared, and she didn't.

'I can't just get up and go to Greece,' she objected. 'I have a job. I work at the Granchester hotel.' She gestured around the small room. 'I live in their staff accommodation.'

'*Neh*, I know. My investigator didn't have to do very much to discover *that*.'

Mia wondered what else his investigator had uncovered. That she lived a simple, almost nun-like existence? That her horizons and ambitions were modest when compared to the high-octane world he undoubtedly inhabited? Had he been surprised when he'd discovered how humble her life had become—or just relieved that he hadn't been forced to endure their farce of a marriage?

She heard another growl of thunder and ran her finger along the neckline of her sticky T-shirt. 'Then you will also know that people rely on me—'

'I'm sure they do,' he interrupted silkily. 'But nobody is indispensable, Mia. Not even you. Tell the hotel you need compassionate leave.' He shrugged. 'If you think it's worth it.'

His words were a challenge and she thought how, in the past, she would have surrendered to his stronger will and been happy to do so—because Theo was a man who seemed to have all the answers, while she had doubted herself all the time. But she wasn't that person any more. She was no longer prepared to accept things on face value, or to always trust somebody else's judgement above her own.

She thought of her grandfather, whose home

had always provided a bright oasis during the few weeks of the school holidays when she'd been permitted to visit him. The man she had adored, despite the vitriol poured into her ear about him by her mother. But he had cut her out of his life as ruthlessly as if she had been a tumour he wanted to excise. She had been disbelieving and hurt—yet part of her had wondered if maybe it was all for the best. At least she didn't have to go back to Greece and see him, and run the risk of bumping into the man she had married.

It had taken a long time for her to realise how much she had missed her grandfather and how much she regretted the rift which had formed between them. No matter what had happened she still loved him—didn't she? Because love, she had discovered, was a remarkably difficult thing to kill off. It clung to the human heart like a baby chimp to its mama. And hadn't one of the lasting regrets of her laughably brief marriage been the rupture in her relationship with him? If he was sick and asking for her, then she needed to go to him.

'Of course I'll come. I'll do whatever it takes,' she said. 'I'll speak to my line manager and arrange a leave of absence, and as soon as I can arrange a ticket, I'll fly out to Athens.'

'Ochi.' He flicked his fingers through the air as if disposing of a troublesome fly. 'You need not

concern yourself with transport, Mia. My plane will be at your disposal.'

'Your *plane*?' All attempts at neutrality forgotten, Mia couldn't keep the disbelief from her voice, finding it hard to reconcile such an obvious symbol of wealth with a man who had first come to the attention of her grandfather when he'd been caught stealing eggs. But even as she said it, she met the glint of something cold and hard in the depths of his black eyes.

'It is something of a transformation, *neh*?' he suggested silkily. 'Or do you still think of me as a man who steals all that comes before him, *zou-zouri mou*?'

'I don't think about you at all,' she said quickly, walking forward to open the window a little wider, as if that would have some kind of magical impact on the stifling atmosphere within the small room.

But the air remained as motionless as before— and all Mia could think of was the way he had tapped so accurately into her thoughts. Which was disturbing. It reminded her of how well Theodoros Aeton had once known her, because she had opened herself up to him in that dumb and trusting way. And she didn't want anyone *knowing* her or having the potential to hurt her. She had become used to her new life and single status. Sometimes it got lonely, but it never got painful. She'd found that animals could love you far better than humans ever could. And wasn't life easier that way? 'I would prefer to travel independently,' she said proudly.

His smile was hard. Almost...wolfish. And annoyingly, it made a ripple of awareness shimmer down the length of her sweat-sheened spine.

'I'm sure you would,' he said. 'But unless you have unlimited time at your disposal, I suggest you accept my offer of a flight and accommodation.'

'Accommodation?' She looked at him blankly. 'You mean, stay with...*you*? I think I'd rather stay with my grandfather.'

He shook his head. 'His house is no place for visitors,' he informed her obliquely. 'And I don't live so far from him.'

Mia swallowed. No, of course he didn't. The two men had often seemed joined at the hip. Sometimes she'd genuinely thought her grandfather preferred the young man he had mentored to his own flesh and blood—*her*. Or maybe that wasn't such a crazy idea. After all, Theo had been an unwanted orphan—a clean slate to write on—while she had always been weighted down by her tainted legacy. The daughter of the son who had disappointed him and the narcissistic woman he should never have married. That she had been an innocent child in a toxic marriage seemed to make no difference to her grandfather. It had taken Mia a long time to realise that she'd never been seen as a person in her own right—just someone who represented the sins of her parents.

But Theo's black gaze was lasering into her and she couldn't seem to shift the erotic images which were suddenly crowding into her head. 'You must be out of your mind,' she breathed, 'if you think I'd ever contemplate staying with *you*.'

'What's your objection? Surely you don't think I will try to persuade you to consummate our marriage, Mia?' His words were a taunt which matched the mirthless quality of his smile. 'I would have thought my track record on sexual restraint speaks for itself.'

Mia could feel the sudden pounding of her heart. 'How can you be so *hateful*?'

'Is it hateful to confront reality?' he challenged. 'I don't think so. And besides, your worries are unnecessary. I live on a property big enough to ensure we need never see one another, unless we choose to.'

'Which is never going to happen!'

His black eyes glittered. 'The alternative is that you find some overheated room in Athens and be forced to rely on taxis to ferry you to and from your grandfather's—a total waste of time and money, which you don't seem to have in any abundance. At least, judging by appearances.' His dark gaze raked around the cramped room as if to add veracity to his words, before shooting an impatient glance at the watch which gleamed gold against his hair-roughened wrist. 'So which is it to be, Mia? I am due at a meeting in precisely forty minutes and have neither the time nor the inclination to hang around here. You have my offer—take it or leave it.'

By the sides of her ancient jeans, Mia curled her fingers into fists, her short, neatly filed nails digging into the palms of her hands.

She ought to hate him. She *did* hate him.

If only her stupid body would stop reacting to him in this debilitating way. Her poor, starving body which had been promised so much pleasure by this man, only to have it snatched away at the eleventh hour.

Theo Aeton's virgin bride had remained a virgin and she'd convinced herself she didn't care.

But it seemed she had been wrong.

Because without doing anything, he had reignited the slow burn of desire, making her realise what she'd been missing during all these long, bleak years. Other men left her cold, but Theo had always been able to make her indecently hot. Was he aware that beneath her creased T-shirt her nipples were becoming hard? Quickly, she crossed her arms over her chest, as the pebbled nubs pressed painfully against the thin cotton. Surely she shouldn't even be *thinking* about such things, when her grandfather was so sick?

But although she was still a virgin, she recognised the importance of sex and, in many ways, the high price tag it carried. And she had few illusions left. In some social circles ancient values prevailed and marriage was still used as a bartering tool. Which was exactly what had happened to her. You could have a mobile phone and a car, you could wear a miniskirt with glittery trainers and walk into a restaurant on your own and nobody would bat an eyelid. But underneath that modern guise, her circumstances had been positively *medieval*. She had been sold by her grandfather to the man in front of her. Traded for a valuable piece of land. A ripe, innocent body exchanged for a metaphorical sack of gold. And nobody had told her about it until it was too late.

Yet things had changed. She was no longer the same naïve woman who had allowed raw teenage emotions to blind her to the truth. She was no longer grateful, or needy, or searching for love in all the wrong places. She would do what she needed to do. The right thing. She wouldn't make a scene, or stubbornly insist on renting some scrubby place miles away from her grandfather's exclusive residence. She would act with pride and dignity as she accepted Theo's offer and visited her aged relative. But she would keep her distance from the man whose wedding ring she had flung deep into the waters of the Ionian sea and watched as it sank without trace. That was the most important thing of all. She must stay away from the Greek billionaire and all the temptation he represented.

'In that case, thank you. I'll speak to my supervisor as soon as you've gone.' Pointedly, she angled her gaze towards the door. 'And find out how soon I can leave.'

He pulled out a small business card and pen from his jacket and she watched as he scrawled something on the back of the card. And suddenly Mia found herself recalling that he hadn't even been able to write his own name until he was fourteen. Who could possibly reconcile that illiterate teenager with this towering man, in his handmade suit and the golden pen which moved so fluidly across the expensive piece of card?

'Let me know when you're able to travel. My office will make all the necessary arrangements. I'll see you on the plane. That's my private number,' he informed her abruptly, as if that were important.

She didn't know what made her say it. A fishing expedition, perhaps? An attempt to discover if there was anyone on the scene and prepare herself for the possibility of a lover's presence on his Greek estate? 'I suppose there are women who would pay a fortune to get their hands on this?'

There was a heartbeat of a pause. 'You'd be surprised,' he said silkily, 'how persistent women can be.'

And Mia knew she had nobody to blame but herself for the shaft of jealousy which stabbed through her.

What were you expecting him to say? That no woman has ever come close to you—the dumpy bride he couldn't even bear to have sex with?

She took the card from him. The brush of his fingers against her own was barely perceptible, yet it was like being touched with fire. Mia could feel the base of her stomach liquefying as memories came flooding back to haunt her with cruel and sensual clarity.

Theo, stripped to the waist and chopping logs, with sweat glittering on his skin like diamonds as he swung an axe through the air.

Theo's fingers straying beneath the lace of her bra, kneading the pliant flesh of her breasts until she was moaning with pleasure.

And Theo kissing her passionately in the moonlight, holding her tightly and telling her he would always respect her.

But those words had been worthless. Each one crumbling to dust as they fell from his lips.

She found out later there had been women before her. Women he had bedded with impunity, unlike her. It had been *her* he had tantalised and teased—leaving her so aching for him that she couldn't think straight. She'd realised afterwards that he must have done it to control her—to make her understand who was in charge. And it had worked, hadn't it? Oh, yes—it had worked, all right.

She needed to be careful.

More than careful.

So she gave the kind of smile she might have bestowed on a nervous new chambermaid on her first day at the Granchester hotel. Friendly yet impartial. As if her pulse weren't thudding erratically at her temple. As if her stomach weren't tying itself up in knots. 'I appreciate you coming here to tell me this—and for offering to help me—but I really need to get changed now.'

'You're going out?' he demanded.

'Yes.'

'With a man?'

Mia wondered how he would react if she confessed that the only person who was longing to see her was Rusty at the dog rescue centre—the ugly little mongrel with the over-long tail. 'That's really none of your business, is it?' she questioned politely.

'Better make sure you take an umbrella.' He directed a glance towards the window, his voice dipping with silky emphasis as he glittered his dark gaze back towards her. 'I'd hate to think of you getting *wet*.'

Mia flushed at the sexual implication, grateful when he turned away, hopefully without noticing her response. As the door closed behind him she could hear his footsteps retreating down the corridor, when suddenly the room was lit by a bright flash of lightning and the sound of thunder crashed through the air.

With sweat still trickling between her breasts, Mia stared out of the window as the long-awaited storm broke.

CHAPTER TWO

THEO TAPPED HIS fingers impatiently against the gleam of his desk as he stared out at the dark sapphire gleam of the Aegean Sea. But for once, he didn't register the dazzling view from the windows of his home office, or the glory of the private beach which lay beyond it. Uncharacteristically, he found himself unable to concentrate on the complex financial negotiations which usually consumed him and which had made him one of the most successful hedge-fund managers on the planet. All he could think about was Mia and the fact that she was due to arrive at any moment.

He wasn't interested in the voicemail message left by a foxy Swedish politician he'd met last month, who'd made it very clear he was her kind of man. Up until a couple of days ago, he had been intending to slot her into his diary—a long weekend in Stockholm or Paris, maybe—though the venue was irrelevant since he doubted they would leave the bedroom. But today such a liaison was the last thing on his mind.

Today, his heart was thudding, his body aching in a way which felt breathtakingly new, yet which haunted the periphery of his senses like the memory of something sweet and mostly forgotten. A pulse began to pound at his temple, because seeing his estranged wife in the flesh a couple of days ago had made him unable to think about anything but her.

His mouth hardened. He had been expecting his duty visit to Mia to give him a sense of closure. Having almost entirely eradicated her from his thoughts, he had imagined his desire for her would have withered when he saw her again, like unpicked grapes on the vine. He tightened his fists and his knuckles cracked, a ghostly white through the olive-darkness of his skin. Because this was a woman who represented his youthful folly and greatest mistake. Whose cruel words on their wedding night had been chosen in order to inflict as much pain as possible and had left a lasting scar upon his heart. He had found that hard to forgive— so it had been easier to forget.

But he had been shocked by the humble circumstances in which he had found her, briefly overwhelmed by a wash of guilt and the knowledge that he had the means to save her from such an existence. But these considerations had been swamped by the unwelcome discovery that his hunger for her hadn't abated, despite her unremarkable appearance. Had he hoped it would? Of course he had. But nobody had ever possessed the power to make him feel the way Mia did.

As if he could explode with lust at any second. As if he had lost temporary control of his senses.

He had left her tiny room, high on a cocktail of lust and jealousy, for hadn't she implied she was meeting someone? Oblivious to the high-powered dealings of his subsequent meeting, he had found himself obsessing about how many men she might have taken to her bed since their split. He knew he was applying the double standards which many men like him were guilty of and, although he knew this was unreasonable intellectually, he found he didn't care. She had implied she was going on a date that day he'd seen her in London. He realised many women enjoyed casual hook-ups, didn't they? And while Theo knew it was old-fashioned to disapprove of such behaviour—he couldn't help himself.

It was the way he'd been brought up.

Or rather, the way he'd *dragged* himself up from the gutter into which he had been born.

Abandoned as a baby, he had been discovered squalling his lungs out in a cardboard box at the roughest end of Athens' main port, Piraeus, on the wettest night of the year. Soaked and starving. It was a wonder he had survived. But survive he had. His mouth hardened into a mirthless smile. Nobody could ever accuse him of a lack of tenacity, or defying the odds. A passing sailor had scooped him up and given him over to the care of a childless, middle-aged woman, who was desperately poor. She had named him Theo Aeton—meaning a gift of God who was as swift as an eagle. Or so she had hoped.

A roof—of sorts—had been provided in exchange for all the food he could bring in as soon as he was old enough to forage. He'd quickly learnt which restaurant bins provided the best bounty—and to get there before the feral cats did. He'd taught himself to fish, and to take tourists around parts of the city which did not feature in their glossy guide books. And even though they sometimes stupidly left their purses gaping open, he never stole their money, for that was a line he would not cross. Need, not greed, had always been his maxim.

Perhaps he would have continued with that hand-to-mouth existence if his 'mother' hadn't died very suddenly, just as most of the city was shutting down for Christmas. Experiencing a grief he hadn't been expecting, which culminated in an urgent need to get away from Athens, Theo had hitched a ride to the luxurious Saronikos gulf, gazing into the lit windows of the beachfront mansions, his stomach rumbling with hunger and his heart aching with envy.

If Mia's grandfather, Georgios Minotis, hadn't caught him stealing eggs, what would have become of him? But nobody had ever been able to answer the conundrum of *'what if?'*, had they?

All Theo knew was that he had faced down the millionaire's wrath with a defiance spurred on by his gnawing hunger. A job had been found for him on the vast estate. He had been put in the servants' quarters and done manual jobs around the place, but after a few months, Georgios had claimed to have seen something special in the boy. A quality he'd never found in his own son—a reckless gambler who had drunk himself to death when his daughter Mia was still a child.

That had been why he'd sent Theo away, to be educated at the finest schools in Europe. Exclusive establishments which initially taught the illiterate boy how to read and write and then, to learn. A thirst for knowledge had been born which had quickly become voracious. Theo's vacations had been spent at different summer schools, acquiring a host of language skills along the way. His winters had seen him skiing in select resorts, mastering first the black runs and then the most treacherous of off-piste skiing. He'd learnt how to ride. Which knife and fork to use at dinner and which fine wines should accompany it. He had learned how to pleasure himself, and the hordes of women eager to share his bed. He'd found himself a job in a bank in Paris and worked there diligently and then, when he was twenty-three years old, he had returned to Saronikos for the summer vacation, at the invitation of his mentor.

And had met the seventeen-year-old Mia.

He had been blown away by her. That voluptuous beauty. The brightness of those blue eyes. She had been holding a wounded puppy, an expression of fierce intent on her face as she'd nursed the mess of his tiny muzzle, for the creature had been injured and blinded in one eye. As she'd lifted her head and their gazes had met, his universe had seemed to shift and realign as he'd recognised something in her which had resonated inside him. Something which had reached out to him. An inner loneliness and a sense of being an outsider. Or at least, that was what he'd allowed himself to believe. His mouth twisted. What a deluded fool he had been. It had been sexual chemistry, pure and simple, given an extra edge by the stark differences in their circumstances. They should have quietly consummated their relationship—the rich girl getting her fulfilment from her experienced *bit of rough*—then gone their separate ways.

But something had held him back and stopped him from satisfying the urgent needs of his body— and hers. An idealism he had not felt before, or since, and which he had been reluctant to put a name to. He had asked her to marry him and when she had accepted, her grandfather had behaved like a man who had just won the jackpot.

So lost was he in his uncomfortable memories that it took a moment for Theo to acknowledge the light tap on his door, which opened on receipt of his terse command, to reveal his housekeeper, Sofia.

'The helicopter is preparing to land, Kyrios Aeton,' she informed him quietly. 'Your guest will be here shortly.'

He could see the curiosity in her lined eyes, because he didn't *usually* request prior warning before a visitor's arrival, nor insist on going to greet them himself. In fact, quite the contrary. Invitations to his private residence were considered such an honour that often guests would be taken to one of the property's many rooms, given a cool drink and asked to enjoy the spectacular view while he finished whatever he was doing, which they seemed happy enough to do. But he did not enlighten the matronly woman who had worked for him for the past five years about the significance of this particular guest. Instead he rose to his feet.

'Efharisto,' he said gruffly, making his way along the cool marble corridors to the main entrance hall and stepping outside into the warmth of the Greek day. But for once he was oblivious

to the potent scent of lemon blossom or the sound of birdsong as he made his way towards the helicopter pad. Instead his eyes were fixed mesmerically on the shiny black craft as it hovered above the pad like a giant insect, before touching down.

The helicopter door opened and there she was with the sun streaming down on her like a spotlight and bathing her in rich gold, her chestnut hair blowing wildly in the upwind. A vision. A pocket-sized goddess—all curves and curls. He ran forward, holding out his hand to assist her, but she shook her head and dismounted the footplates herself, clinging onto the billowing skirt of her dress with one hand, as if her life depended on it.

'This way,' he shouted, above the sound of the engine, and she nodded as they made their way towards the house.

Sofia must have left the front door open, but Mia stood in front of it without moving—as if the hounds of hell were contained within its white portals. Theo glanced down at her and as she met his gaze her expression was one he didn't recognise—for it was wary and fierce. And he could do nothing about the sudden tightening of his body as his gaze drank her in. Today she wasn't wearing a pair of old jeans and a T-shirt which had badly needed ironing, but had replaced them with a pretty dress which emphasised her voluptuous shape. Her full lips bore the soft sheen of pink lipstick and Theo felt a sudden rush of heat, as desire began to beat its way insistently through his veins.

'Mia,' he said, unable to prevent the husky timbre of his voice.

Mia felt her throat dry. Don't say my name that way, she wanted to plead. And don't look at me like that, either. Because that sultry tone and molten gaze didn't mean anything. They never had. They were just weapons in his armoury of seduction and he used them well. Theo had always been a master at making her feel what he'd wanted her to feel. He had used her. Big time. And she should forget that at her peril.

'I don't know why you're looking so surprised,' she said, hitching the strap of her shoulder bag and fixing him with a cool smile. 'You were the one who sent your plane for me and then a helicopter to pick me up from the airfield, which I thought was slightly over the top. Surely you hadn't forgotten I was coming, Theo? Although...'

'Mmm?' he prompted, his ebony gaze fixed to her mouth as her words tailed off. 'Although what?'

Mia hesitated, but her determination to remain immune to him was proving near impossible. It was hard to concentrate when he'd left the top two buttons of his shirt undone like that. Had he done that deliberately? Exposed an enticing glimpse of olive skin, which gleamed like oiled silk, inviting the touch of her suddenly restless fingers? It was a terrible distraction and so was the way he was looking at her. But you could hardly ask a man to avert his gaze because you didn't like the way it made you *feel*, could you? It had taken all her resolve to agree to stay in his house and it wasn't going to do her frazzled nerves any good if she went to pieces every time she was close to him.

Her tongue flicked out to moisten a mouth which had grown uncomfortably dry. 'I was expecting you to be on the flight with me from England,' she croaked. 'At least, that's what you said to me in London.'

'I know I did.' He shrugged. 'But something came up.'

She almost said, *And you didn't bother to tell me?* before reminding herself that she, of all people, had no right to sound like a nagging wife.

'I had to fly to Paris last night on business and it made sense to come straight on here this morning.' His gaze was mocking. 'And I thought you'd be pleased at the thought of travelling alone.'

'Obviously.' Mia certainly wasn't going to admit that when he hadn't shown up, she had experienced something which had felt weirdly like *disappointment*. It was one thing to convince herself that she hadn't wanted to endure three and a half hours of Theo's company during a claustrophobic flight to Athens. Quite another to have that option removed without her knowledge, leaving her feeling distinctly wrong-footed when the stewardess had sashayed into the plane's plush interior to inform her that her boss wouldn't be coming after all.

'Where is he?' The words had shot from Mia's mouth before she could stop them and she'd been unable to miss the woman's look of surprise—presumably at her daring to ask such a direct question. She wondered how much more surprised the stewardess would be to discover that Mia was actually the legal *wife* of the boss!

But nobody knew—a decision they both seemed to have arrived at, without prior consultation. She had never once used his name and had noticed there was no mention of her in his biography. It was weird, really—how easily you could be airbrushed from someone's life. Had it been easy for him to forget the plump teenage bride who had provided him with a prestigious piece of the Greek coastline?

Was that the reason why she had dressed for the journey with the kind of care she hadn't taken for ages, because he'd caught her looking so scruffy when he'd turned up the other day? Admittedly, her navy and white dress was a little snug around the hips, and her espadrilles could have done with a new set of ribbons, but her hair was freshly washed and the red-brown curls were bouncing around her shoulders. She'd even applied a little make-up and dabbed on a slick of lipstick. And then, when she'd learned about his no-show, she had felt like a little girl who had dressed up for a party and got the date wrong. As if she'd tried too hard.

But there was nothing wrong with taking a little trouble with her appearance, she reasoned. It was what most women did every day of their lives. Usually, she dressed casually during her downtime, because the dogs at the rescue centre left her covered in hair, but that didn't rule out an occasional change. It certainly didn't mean that she was trying to ensnare Theo Aeton, or make herself more attractive to him. Of course it didn't.

She forced herself to remember the reason she was here. The *only* reason.

'How is my grandfather?' she questioned.

'I spoke to his nurse this morning. He's stable. I'm planning to go and see him this afternoon—'

'Can I come with you?' she said quickly.

'That's something we need to discuss. But not on the doorstep. Do you want to come inside, Mia?' he questioned, pulling the door open a little wider. 'Or just stand there, looking decorative?'

Decorative? Mia frowned at his choice of word. Was that a good or a bad thing? She wasn't sure. It made her think of a Christmas tree. She glanced back in the direction of the helicopter pad. 'My luggage—'

'Someone will take care of that and bring it to your room.'

'How comfortable you sound, with all your servants,' she observed wryly.

'Hopefully the people who work for me are just as comfortable. I try never to forget I was once a servant myself.' His mouth twisted into a mocking smile. 'As people like you were so keen to remind me.'

My, how the tables had turned, Mia thought as she stepped over the threshold and looked around the entrance hall, trying to take in the opulence of her surroundings. Their roles had been completely reversed, she realised. He had a mansion, while she lived in a poky rented room. He was rich and she was poor and it was…well, it was more than a little disconcerting.

She had been gobsmacked as the helicopter had skirted a private beach, then hovered over massive, flower-filled grounds containing a huge blue swimming pool, shaped like a T. Her lips had curved with slight derision when she'd seen *that*. They had flown over a modern house—a vast steel and glass construction bathed in different shades of blue as it reflected the sky and sea. And Mia had realised with a sense of disbelief that this was Theo's property. Or rather, Theo's estate, with its olive and lemon groves, which were obviously commercially farmed. He owned the lot.

And all because of her.

All because of her.

Her inheritance had provided this for him. The land he had acquired when he'd signed the wedding certificate must have financed it all. No wonder he could afford to look smug. But no way was she going to be bitter, because there was no point. She had turned her back on the old life. She didn't need vast wealth. She'd seen the unhappiness and discontentedness it could bring and was happier with her modest goals. She certainly wasn't going to start doing checks and balances, or comparing her lifestyle to that of the towering billionaire in front of her.

She didn't even want to think about Theo, in those dark trousers which moulded his powerful thighs and a silk shirt the pale, creamy colour of raspberry yoghurt, which hinted distractingly at the rocky torso beneath. So she smiled politely, just as she might have done if she were being shown around a stately home in England, searching for something appropriate to say. 'Mmm… Very impressive,' she said. 'The modern architecture works really well against this landscape.'

His eyes narrowed, as if her cool deliberation had come as something of a surprise. 'Let me show you the rest.'

She shook her head. 'No, honestly, that won't be necessary, Theo. There must be someone else you can ask. I'm sure there are much more important calls on your time than having to act as an unofficial guide to me.'

'Possibly, but I prefer never to delegate tasks which could be potentially troublesome. And unless your Greek has improved dramatically and as nobody speaks English as fluently as I do,' he added, his eyes glittering with unholy humour, 'it seems you're stuck with me.'

'Is your swimming pool really shaped like the initial of your name?' she questioned archly, intending to goad him. 'I couldn't believe it when I saw a giant T. The ego has landed! Are there monograms on your towels, or woven into the rugs?'

But he didn't take the bait, his lazy shrug indicating he was unmoved by her sarcasm. 'My architect persuaded me it would be a good idea. The vertical part of the T is a lane pool designed for swimming lengths, which I do every morning, and the horizontal bar is the infinity part, which overlooks the sea. It's a practical design rather than being done for reasons of status,' he concluded drily before beckoning her. 'Come.'

Slightly irritated by his imperious command and her mind now stuck in an annoying groove of imagining Theo swimming, Mia was left with little option but to follow him, trying to take it all in as he showed her around the sprawling villa. The huge rooms. The white walls. The bold oil paintings which added bright pops of colour. Butter-soft leather sofas occupied light-filled spaces and there were several glass tables on which stood exquisite pieces of blue china. Yet as she looked around, she found herself thinking this was no place for a child. Was that intentional? She wondered what would happen if—when—he met a woman he might want to make babies with and the thought upset her more than it should have done.

She still didn't know if there was anyone in his life. Maybe she should ask him for a divorce— wasn't it time one of them did that? That would be the most diplomatic way of finding out about his personal circumstances and might spur her into taking action to formally end their sexless union. She swallowed. Unless she was intending to continue in this strange marital limbo of theirs for ever.

In an attempt to lose her uncomfortable preoccupation, Mia turned her attention to the gardens, which they had just entered via a vine-covered veranda. The sunlit grounds were very beautiful and, despite her barbed comments, the swimming pool was even more impressive when seen from the ground. The glassy blue water shimmered invitingly as Mia tried to remember the last time she'd swum anywhere which wasn't an echoey public bath which smelt strongly of chlorine.

'It looks fabulous,' she said.

Theo inclined his black head. 'Use it whenever you want.'

'Thanks.'

He introduced her to a cook who was doing something complicated with filo pastry in the kitchen and to Sofia, his housekeeper, saying something in Greek too rapid for Mia to understand—she caught the word for lemon, but her grasp of the language had always been superficial and her mother had actively discouraged her from speaking it.

But once they had mounted the wide marble staircase and found themselves alone on the first floor of the enormous villa, Mia turned to him curiously, hating the way her gaze was drawn so irrevocably to the sculpted lines of his lips. Hating even more her sudden burning wish to have those lips kiss her again. She hesitated. 'What did you tell Sofia?'

He knitted his dark brows together. 'I said we might drink some lemon *pressé* on one of the terraces once I'd shown you around.'

'No, not then,' she said, more crossly than she had intended. 'I mean, what have you told her about me?'

Theo felt a beat of irritation, turning away from

the question in her blue eyes, and continued to walk along the upper level of the house. He heard her follow, her footsteps light on the silken rug, but his pace didn't slacken until he reached a suite which had been chosen deliberately because it was the furthest from his own. His mouth hardened. He didn't want her accusing him of using proximity to his advantage. More importantly, he didn't want to put any temptation in his way.

Throwing open the door of the airy chamber, he walked inside. 'This is yours.'

'Does she know? Sofia, I mean,' she persisted, paying absolutely no attention to her surroundings. 'Who around here is aware that I'm your wife, Theo?'

He turned around to meet a stubborn expression he didn't recognise, forcing him to acknowledge she had changed. They had both changed, he realised. 'Very few people know.' His mouth twisted. 'A failed marriage isn't something I tend to boast about. I prefer to focus on my successes, not my failures.'

'What about my grandfather's staff?'

'There is nobody left there who knows you.'

'Nobody at all?' she questioned, with a frown. 'Not even Elena, or Christos?'

'They have all gone,' he said coolly. 'His life is very different now, Mia. When he first became ill, he withdrew from everything he knew. In many ways he adopted the life of a hermit. Against my advice, he dismissed all his permanent employees and now a skeleton of temporary staff keep him and the place ticking over—just about.' His gaze became narrowed. 'My own staff have been acquired within the last five years, and, to all intents and purposes, regard me as a single man.'

There was a pause. 'And do you behave like a single man, Theo?' she said quietly.

It was a question he hadn't been expecting and Theo felt himself tense. A pulse began to beat at his temple, and somewhere else, too. He was hard now, just as he'd been hard when he'd seen her in London. He shifted his weight. 'Are you asking me whether I've had sex with other women since we've been apart, Mia?' he queried huskily. 'Because, to echo your own words, that's really none of your business.'

'Of course I'm not,' she answered hastily. 'I just wanted to know...'

As her words tailed off Theo thought of all the questions she could have asked him. Things like: had he ever really loved her, or had he just done it for the money? Or, even more crucially, had he ever regretted never having consummated their relationship? Which, of course, he had, more times than he cared to remember. Questions she'd never asked at the time but which he had little appetite to answer now, because surely they were as inconsequential as the leaves which fell from the autumn trees before drying to dust on the ground.

As was she.

But suddenly she didn't seem so inconsequential. Not when she was here, in his house, and his long-repressed fantasy of having her alone in a bedroom was actually being realised. The breath had caught in his throat and suddenly he was having to steel himself against the powerful impact she was having on his senses.

His throat dried as his hungry gaze drank her in. Those big blue eyes and the coppery tangle of her curls. And her body. How could he have forgotten that voluptuous body, which he had denied himself for reasons which now seemed like insanity?

He could see the sudden tremble of her lips and read the desire which was darkening her eyes. A desire as heavy as the atmosphere just before the storm which had broken when he'd left her room in London, leaving his shirt and jacket saturated with rain and clinging to his chest.

He could hear the thunder of his heart and he was so caught up with the idea of having sex with her that his words became a taunt, intended more as a provocation than because he was particularly interested in hearing the answer.

'What do you want to know, Mia?' he demanded softly. 'Ask me anything you want and I'll tell you.'

She tilted her chin, but not—as he had hoped—as a silent invitation to kiss her. No, her mouth had tightened, not softened, and her bald words shattered the sensual bubble which had surrounded him.

'Why have you never asked me for a divorce?'

His lips hardened into a cynical smile. Why did she think? That he was a sentimentalist, who believed in the sanctity of marriage above all else? Or that he was holding out hope that she might return to him, so that they could start a family of their own?

'Interesting you should say that,' he mused, dampening down the tumult of his thoughts and replacing them with the cool logic which had given him such a formidable reputation in the boardroom. 'When I've been thinking exactly the same thing. Because you are the one who has everything to gain from a legal termination of our marriage, Mia.' He paused. 'So why have *you* never asked for a divorce?'

CHAPTER THREE

MIA GAVE A click of irritation as Theo's lips twisted into a hard smile, because he *always* did this. She had asked him a question and he had turned it back on her. He used language not as a form of communication but as a barrier—and a weapon. And he did it in five different languages! He was too clever for his own good, she thought resentfully.

Yet hadn't that always been one of the things she had so admired about him—the way he'd embraced learning so eagerly, even though he had started so much later than anyone else? He had behaved as if education was a privilege and an honour, not a right or a burden. He had seemed to know everything, while she had known nothing—or so it had seemed at the time.

Meeting the dark gleam of his eyes, she attempted to answer his question without giving too much away. Because somehow that was important.

As if revealing how badly he had hurt her would make her feel vulnerable, all over again.

'There was no reason for me to seek a divorce,' she explained.

'Really?' He raised his brows. 'Even though your life is far more humble than your beginnings must have prepared you for? The man you married is now a billionaire, Mia—'

'Would you like a quick round of applause?'

'Which means any judge would award you the kind of settlement which would keep you more than comfortable for the rest of your life,' he continued, unperturbed, though he gave a flicker of a smile as his gaze travelled over her flushed face. 'You wouldn't have to work in a hotel and live in a room not much bigger than a cloakroom.'

'You think that money is the answer to everything?' she demanded. 'Is that the god you worship?' She turned away to look out of the window—not because she wanted to appreciate the sapphire slash of the sea, or the creamy froth of the distant citrus orchard, but because she didn't want him to see the prick of tears in her eyes. How annoying that he could cut right through her defences, almost without trying. Quickly, she blinked them away, waiting until she had composed herself, before turning to face him again. 'I suppose you must do, since you were prepared to marry me in order to get your hands on the stuff!'

But he didn't rise to the insult.

'How easy it is for people to be dismissive of the power of money, when they've been cushioned by wealth all their lives,' he offered coolly.

She was conscious of his gaze raking over her unruly curls. 'I didn't have wealth,' she defended hotly. 'Not really. You met me on one of my annual visits to see my grandfather—you had no idea what my life was like back in England.'

There was a pause. 'So why don't you tell me what it was like?'

The question took her by surprise, because it sounded as if he really wanted to know. As if he were genuinely interested in her background, in a way he'd never been before. Why had that been? How could they have agreed to marry when they'd known so little about each other?

Because they'd both been on a high—too preoccupied with the fluctuation of youthful hormones and the lure of the sex he seemed intent on denying her.

Facts had taken second place to feelings and she had been completely captivated by those. Mia tried to cast her mind back to a young woman blinded by need and romantic illusion—and that person was someone she could barely recognise.

'Yes, we lived in a big house but it had hardly any furniture in it,' she said slowly. 'Because my father gambled away most of his inheritance and after he died, my mother frittered away what little was left. So my grandfather paid my school fees and arranged for grocery deliveries to be made. He provided all the basics, but nothing more.' She shrugged. 'And my mother resented him because she wanted more. It's why she used to let me come over and stay with him during the summer holidays, even though she hated him. She thought I might be able to soften him up. Her dream was that I would return to England with a fistful of euros. But that never happened.'

'Your grandfather has many assets,' he observed thoughtfully. 'But cash has never been one of them. Most of his wealth is tied up in the land.'

'As I was soon to discover for myself,' she said, the sharp reminder of his betrayal making her forget her determination not to be bitter.

'Mia—'

'No!' she interjected, with a fierce shake of her head. 'You asked me a question and you need to hear my answer without any attempts to absolve yourself.'

'Absolve myself?' he echoed.

'That's what I said!' But defiance was a newfound weapon in her armoury and it took a little getting used to, and Mia found herself sinking onto a leather seat, her legs feeling strangely wobbly 'I met you that summer when I was seventeen and I'd...'

'What?' he prompted softly as her words tailed off.

She thought about sugar-coating it. About making it sound as if it had meant nothing. But that would be a lie told to salvage her own ego. And hadn't she lost enough already because of her failed marriage? Surely the truth shouldn't be another casualty.

'I'd never felt like that about anyone before,' she admitted. 'Perhaps because I'd never really had the chance to meet any men. Despite my mother having been a model, I'd led quite a sheltered life and went to an all-girls school.' She pulled a face. 'And, like I said, there was never enough cash to splash on school trips or new clothes, so I was always the odd one out.' There had been another reason for her almost hermit-like lifestyle, which had little to do with poverty. Because the willowy ex-supermodel who had given birth to Mia could never quite get her head around having produced such an ugly duckling of a child. The little girl who had been intended as an accompaniment to complement her mother's remarkable beauty had been hidden away at home—while all methods intended to improve her appearance had been doomed to disappoint.

If she tried—which these days she never did—

she could still hear her mother's tinkling English accent as she'd trilled out her various observations.

Surely you're not going to eat *that*? No wonder you're so chubby, darling!

If you don't move a bit more, Mia, then you'll *never* get rid of that spare tyre!

'I know you married me to get the land, Theo. I know that,' Mia reiterated. 'And it sort of makes sense now. I couldn't understand at the time why someone like you…who could have had anyone… should have wanted…me,' she finished, trying very hard not to gulp.

He stared at her and the silence which followed seemed to go on for a very long time. 'Your mother told you that, did she?'

Swallowing down the lump in her throat, Mia nodded as the hateful words came spiralling back down the years.

Surely you don't think a man like Theodoros Aeton would marry a little fatty like you, if he weren't being paid?

'She told me when I was changing for the evening party.' Mia hadn't thought it possible to hurt that much. To feel as if a knife had ripped open her chest and a ragged-nailed hand had reached inside the gaping cavity to tear her heart out. She'd been standing in front of a full-length mirror at the time, in her too-tight white wedding dress. She had felt like a white, bloated maggot and she had looked like it, too.

'And you believed her?' Theo demanded.

'Why wouldn't I? She told me you'd struck a deal with my grandfather.'

His gaze was very steady, but there was a glint of something hard and bitter in the depths of those black eyes. 'But you didn't stop to find out my side of the story, did you, Mia? That didn't occur to you?'

Mia chewed on her lip. Of course she hadn't. How could she explain how naïve she'd felt when the facts had fallen into place and she'd finally understood why the most devastatingly gorgeous man she'd ever laid eyes on had asked her to be his wife? If he'd explained from the outset that he was courting her because it was financially advantageous for him to do so, then maybe she could have accepted it. She had adored him so much that she thought she would have accepted whatever scraps he deigned to throw her. But he hadn't. He had spun his silken words like a spider spinning a golden web and she had become enmeshed in them. So she had melted when he'd husked into her ear that he'd never desired a woman as much as her. He hadn't mentioned love, but that hadn't seemed to matter. Because she'd believed in her love for *him*, imagining she had enough for both of them and it was strong enough to withstand anything fate had in store for them. But she had fallen at the first hurdle, because betrayal and deceit were powerful weapons when you held them up against something as fragile as love.

'Why bother,' she questioned, her words tinged with acid, 'when it was true?'

Theo felt the erratic pound of his heart as impatience vied with an anger which had suddenly become red-raw. Surely she should know that life was never that cut and dried. But facts were facts and he couldn't change them now. On one level he had been aware that she had idolised him more than was healthy, but she had been so sweet about it that he had accepted it. He hadn't wanted to crush her dreams, because in a way he had been caught up in them himself—for the first and last time in his life.

And she had been vulnerable. Like a small shoot pushing its way up towards the light, she had needed careful nurturing. It had been the only time Theo had ever met a woman who had been totally without agenda. She had been warm and giving. Her ripe innocence had been her both her strength and her shield and, from the start, he had felt an overpowering protectiveness towards her. His simplistic view of what constituted a 'good' woman had been personified in the curly-headed virgin who had responded so passionately to his kisses.

And so he had waited—even though it had half killed him to do so. His determination not to possess her fully until she was his wife had driven him. It had been yet one more achievement to add to his list.

'I agreed to what was, in effect, a dowry,' he said slowly, 'because I knew that unless I did so, your grandfather would refuse to let me have your hand in marriage.'

'Oh, how very admirable!' Those Aegean eyes sparked blue fire at him. 'So you did it out of the goodness of your heart?'

'Think about it,' he came back at her. 'I was a modestly paid bank worker at the time—certainly not able to keep you in the manner in which you deserved to be kept!'

'I am not an animal, I don't need to be *kept*,' she retorted, her voice shaking. 'I didn't need his land. I didn't want it!'

'And neither did I,' Theo ground out, the words rushing from his lips like a swollen river breaking through the banks and suddenly he realised how long he had repressed this. All this time he had lived with the knowledge that she'd thought so little of him and it seemed she still did. He felt the fierce fire of injustice and allowed the cold swamp of anger to blot it out. 'Don't you know why he did it, Mia? Why he made me that offer?'

Silently, Mia shook her head, taken aback by the sudden bitterness in his voice.

'Because he thought if he gifted you the land, then your mother would manipulate you and wrangle it away from you.' His gaze bored into her like a dark laser. 'And subsequently sell some of the most valuable coastal real estate in Greece to some disreputable property developer, who would fill the place with high-rise hotels and turn this haven of a place into a tacky holiday destination. Can you imagine what that would have been like? All this beauty which surrounds us vanquished, and in its place all-day breakfasts and happy hours.'

Her breath was coming thick and fast and as Mia stared at him uncomprehendingly, the world as she knew it was suddenly upended. 'Why didn't you tell me this before?'

'Because I was waiting for our wedding night, when we would finally be alone. As your husband, I was planning to sign it all over to you. Every. Damned. Acre. But you didn't stop to ask, did you?' His mouth twisted into a bitter line. 'You just assumed I was bad and greedy and manipulative. It was as though you'd been waiting for something like this to happen. Something to condemn me in your eyes.'

And to her shame, Mia couldn't deny his words. She *had* been in a state of disbelief. She hadn't believed it possible that a person could make her feel as good as Theo did and of *course* she had suspected his motives from time to time. Her mother's carping criticisms had worn her down over the years, like the drip-drip of water against the walls of a cave. She'd accepted all those negative assessments about her appearance because, deep down, she'd known they were true. She *was* dumpy and dull. She *was* a very average pupil at school. She had been angry with Theo for having deceived her, but even angrier with herself for allowing herself to be such a pathetically easy target. And that anger and hurt had fuelled the words she had flung at him.

'Do you remember what you said to me that night?' he questioned coldly, again tapping uncomfortably into her thoughts.

She bit her lip so hard she could taste the metallic slick of blood. Of course she could remember. No matter how hard she'd tried to forget, fragments of those accusations had remained in the recesses of her mind—branded like fire onto her memory. She had hissed at him like a cornered possum. Told him he had let himself down and shown his true colours. That his gutter mentality had come to the fore and thank goodness she had found out in time. And she hadn't stopped there. She'd been high on fear and rage and hurt, and the words had continued to come rushing out in a vitriolic spill. Words she hadn't really understood but which she realised afterwards must have been spoken by her mother and she must have subconsciously soaked them all up, like a sponge. She had accused him of being a fortune-hunter. A thief. And a gigolo. It had been that single word which had caused the final rupture before she had run off into the night. She had seen him recoil, and his mouth flatten with a look she'd never seen before, but once the anger had fled from his black eyes, he had recovered his composure with remarkable speed.

'Hardly a gigolo, *zouzouri mou*,' he had drawled, somehow managing to make the formerly tender endearment into a vicious insult. 'I didn't actually have *sex* with you in exchange for the land—no matter how many times you begged me to.'

Something had twisted and died inside her—was it her hopes and her dreams, or just the realisation that she had been punching above her weight all along?

Mia had fled from the room. Even now the memory of his response made her want to run away again. She would have given anything to have escaped Theo's modern mansion and the teeming painful memories and the penetrating gleam of his black eyes. But where would she go? She had accepted his hospitality in order to see her dying grandfather. She mustn't let his words get to her. He shouldn't still have that power over her.

She turned from his dark gaze to stare out of the window again, oblivious to the bluebell tint of the sky. 'I should have stayed right here and faced the music,' she said, and couldn't stop herself from wondering if the outcome would have been different if she had done. Would she have remained as his wife if she had been honest with him? His *real* wife? Would they have created the family she'd longed for, the family she'd never really had? A dark wave of longing washed over her and she had to swallow down the lump in her throat before she could continue. 'But I was young,' she husked.

'We were both young,' he said, his voice gravel-hard. 'Tell me what you did next.'

'I went back to England,' she said slowly. 'And realised there was no way I could carry on living with my mother. Anyway, she'd met a rich American by then. A sugar daddy. Her words, not mine.' She gave a short laugh. 'So she went to Florida to live with him, hoping he would marry her, though he never has.'

'And you? What did you do, Mia?'

She shrugged. 'I needed independence and to find my own way in the world, but of course I had no money.'

'Not quite so straightforward without the cushion of cash, is it, *zouzouri mou*?' His lips curved. 'Weren't you tempted to come back, to ask for some proceeds from the estate? Or to demand that I sell up the land and give you the proceeds?'

'With my tail between my legs? *Begging* you?' she questioned proudly. 'Never in a million years! I'd had it with that kind of life, Theo, so I decided to do what most people in that position do. I started looking for a job and, since I didn't have very much in the way of qualifications, I found one as a maid.'

'A maid?' he echoed.

The disbelief in his voice was unmistakable and it riled her, because hadn't she encountered this kind of prejudice time and time again? 'It's a very worthwhile job,' she defended staunchly. 'Creating order out of chaos and enhancing people's enjoyment of their stay. Nobody's ever going to object if someone else is making their bed for them, are they? I mean, there are a lot of…um…' she pulled a face '…unsavoury things which people leave in their rooms, but mostly—I liked it.'

'So you left me standing at the altar in order to become a maid?' He gave a cynical laugh. 'I suppose I should be offended, but instead I find it rather…*amusing*. Tell me—does your grandfather know about the unexpected career you have chosen?'

'He wouldn't take my phone calls, and he never answered any of my letters, so I don't know if he read them. I suppose I must just be grateful that he wants to see me now.'

His expression suddenly became closed and he crossed the room to open the French doors, which led out onto a large and leafy terrace. And although Mia told herself she was grateful he'd put some distance between them, the change of perspective was making her aware of things she'd been trying very hard not to focus on before.

Emphasised by the bright sunlight streaming in from behind him, his body was outlined with heart-stopping definition. Through the fine material of his silk shirt the musculature of his broad-shouldered back was plainly visible. Against her will, her gaze travelled over the powerful shafts of his long legs and the ebony gleam of his thick hair. As she watched him, she could feel a silken flicker begin to pulse deep inside her. Her heart was jumping all over the place and her cheeks felt hot and flushed. Mia told herself she should be over him by now—so why was her stubborn body refusing to listen? As he turned round, did he catch her practically drooling over him? Was that why his eyes glinted with dark fire?

Suddenly, she was pathetically grateful to hear a tap on the door. 'Who's that?' she questioned hoarsely.

Theo tensed, not wanting to be disturbed and sorely tempted to demand that the caller go away.

'Ela,' he said tersely and the door opened to admit Dimitra, his maid, the daughter of his gardener. She was new to the job and very nervous as she deposited Mia's suitcase in the centre of the room, before scuttling out again. Almost immediately, Sofia appeared, carrying a jug of lemon *pressé* and two frosted glasses on a tray, which she placed on a table beside the window, correctly interpreting his almost imperceptible shake of the head, before slipping quietly from the room.

And then he and Mia were alone again—facing each other like strangers and acting as if there weren't a huge bed within tumbling distance. Theo stared at the woman he had married—at the curves of her firm flesh, which were drenched with golden sunlight—and felt the beat of something he didn't recognise. Was it frustration? 'You will have something to drink?' he questioned, finding himself in the unfamiliar position of waiting on someone.

She nodded. 'Sure.'

Ice cubes chinking, he carried the cordial across the room to her, watching her mouth pursing as she sucked a long draft of *pressé* through the glass straw, leaving her lips gleaming and wet. She wasn't being deliberately provocative—at least he didn't think she was—but there was something about her fresh beauty which made watching her feel like a necessity rather than a choice. As she took another gulp, her head was bent, showcasing those snaky spirals of copper which had always given her that faintly wanton appearance—which was ironic, given that she had been so innocent. Six years on, she was unlikely to have remained a virgin and the thought of her being with other men was unendurable. He tensed as a fierce pain twisted darkly at his heart.

As she raised her eyes and caught him watching her, something in the air seemed to shift and change. Something raw and powerful which, when Theo thought about it afterwards, had seemed inevitable from the moment she had set foot inside his house.

He moved towards her and, taking the half-drunk glass from her unprotesting fingers, heard her sharp intake of breath. Her eyes were unblinking and her lips tremulous as he stared at her for a very long time, as if mulling over his options—and hers—before pulling her into his arms.

And she let him. Actually, that was a lie. She didn't just *let* him—she melted into his waiting embrace as if she was powerless to stop herself. As if she had been waiting for this to happen for as long as he had.

How long was that?

Since he'd walked into that cramped and muggy room in London and found her looking hot and crumpled, with sweat gleaming like polish on her clammy skin? Or when she'd arrived here this afternoon with that summery dress swirling around the undulation of her hips and her curls glinting like bright fire in the sunlight. His lips flattened. Or maybe this was the same seed of hunger which had been planted a long time ago. Planted and then left to wither and die.

But it hadn't died. It must have been growing stealthily inside him all this time and now it was all-consuming. It was heating his blood and making his senses raw. It was hardening his groin. Unbearably.

He moved his face closer to hers and saw her eyes grow dark—two pools of fathomless ebony fixed on his. Her lips were parted and even though those plump, pink cushions had always tantalised him, he did not kiss her immediately, even though invitation was screaming from every pore of her body. He allowed himself a heartbeat longer, seeing the sudden confusion on her face. A wave of something like satisfaction washed over him as he welcomed the familiar mantle of power—of being the one in the driving seat. Thank God for his legendary control, he thought grimly. That steely control which he had never needed more than he did right now.

'You want this?' he said, his question almost careless.

Those Aegean eyes narrowed and she seemed to hesitate before she nodded—as if she wanted to demonstrate that she had power, too. But he saw the capitulation in her eyes the moment it happened—and the hunger, too. The sharp, intense hunger which easily matched his own.

'Yes,' she answered, almost angrily. *'Yes.'*

CHAPTER FOUR

THERE WAS NO finesse in Theo's kiss. No build-up, or teasing, or provocation. His lips were urgent and hungry and although Mia instantly responded to the hot, hard pressure of his lips, she couldn't stem the frantic questions which rushed into her mind.

Why was she letting this happen?

Why?

But it was a long time since she had kissed anyone and it seemed that sexual frustration was a powerful driver. Much too powerful to resist—and she had never had much luck resisting Theo anyway. With a little moan she opened her lips, kissing him back with clumsy need but also with a kind of despair. Because she didn't *want* to feel like this. As if he were consuming her and dominating every single one of her senses, until all she could think about was him and only him. She didn't want to make those swooning little sounds as he flicked his tongue inside her mouth, as if he *owned* it or something. Or squirm with frustration as her breasts met the rocky resistance of his chest. And she definitely didn't want to part her legs to allow one powerful leg to slide between her trembling thighs.

But she did all those things. She did them with a fervour which shocked her, no matter how loudly her conscience was clamouring in her ears. Already she felt out of control, while Theo seemed in total command of himself. He whispered his fingertips all the way down her back and then tangled them proprietorially in her hair, cupping the back of her head with his hand so that he could increase the pressure on her mouth.

How could a kiss be so incredible, she wondered dazedly, and how long did it last? She couldn't tell. Not when time seemed to be playing tricks on her. Suddenly she didn't *care* about the lack of romance and affection. It didn't seem to matter, because a kiss could make past and present merge into one blissful whole and make you feel happy again, couldn't it? It could make you remember what it felt like to be alive and in love. Was that why she pressed her breasts so brazenly against him? And why his palms cupped her buttocks to bring her up against the cradle of his pelvis, so that she could feel the unashamed outline of his arousal.

'Oh, God,' she breathed in wonder as he circled his hips against hers very deliberately.

'I want you,' he said, with cool calculation as he drew away from her. 'Can you feel how much?'

His words should have shocked her, but they did no such thing. They thrilled her. They made her want more. 'You kn-know I can,' she answered brokenly. 'Y-you're so big. So h-hard.'

Was it her stumbled response which made him shudder like that?

'Mia,' he said, breaking the kiss to suck in a great gulp of breath, as if to replenish his oxygen-starved lungs. *'Evge...!'*

That Greek exclamation she knew—an expression of praise she'd heard him use in the past—but the other words which were falling from his lips were a mystery. Not just because of her lack of fluency but because his rough tone was making them almost incomprehensible. Was he flattering her, or damning her? It sounded like a mixture of both.

But she didn't care. How could she care about anything other than this...? *This.* The thumb which was grazing over her cotton-covered nipple was unsteady and the groan he gave as he buried his mouth in her hair made him sound as if he had temporarily lost control.

So what if he had?

Hadn't she?

Wasn't this the best thing that had happened to her in six long years?

His mouth was on her jaw.

And then drifting downwards.

She could feel the warmth of his breath against her skin. He was whispering kisses down her neck, until he reached the scalloped edge of her sundress. Holding her breath with anticipation, Mia could feel her swollen breasts pushing towards his lips, bullet-like nipples sending out a silent scream for him to bare them, or touch them, or do *something* rather than leave her aching like this.

Did he realise how wet she was? Was that why he began to ruck up her skirt with a low laugh of triumph? That should have been enough to make her stop, but her starved senses were refusing to let her. She could feel his hand tiptoeing up over her leg and the goose-bumping of tender skin as he edged towards the juncture of her thighs. And now came the light graze of his finger—negligent, almost careless—as it skated over the engorged mound of her panties.

Mia gasped, her eyelids fluttering to a close because his finger was moving against the silk-covered bud with exquisite accuracy and the scent of her arousal was filling the air with musky perfume. She was parting her thighs, eager for him to push aside the damp fabric and caress her heated flesh. Or maybe to tug the unwanted panties down and let them flutter to her ankles like a white silk flag of surrender. Already, she was close. So close.

And Mia knew if she didn't call a halt to this, something was going to happen.

She froze. Not just *something*. Any minute now and she would be gasping out a helpless orgasm, administered by a cold-blooded man who had made no secret of his contempt for her. What would *that* do for her feelings of self-worth? She wasn't a teenager any more, whose sexual response was being governed by a man who liked to control. *She* was the one in charge of her own body and she couldn't let this happen.

She didn't say a word. She didn't have to. He must have correctly interpreted her wishes because he let his hand fall, before quickly walking away from her as if her touch had begun to contaminate him. His shoulders were hunched, his ragged breathing the only sound breaking the fraught silence. Her heart thundering, Mia surveyed the forbidding set of his body as she tried to rationalise what had happened, feeling as if some sort of explanation was required. As if she needed to say something which would rid her of the stupid certainty that she had just passed up on a piece of paradise. A few words which might help claw back what little remained of her dignity.

'We…we shouldn't have done that.'

'Parakalo,' he said coolly, holding up the palm of his hand, like a city policeman stopping the traffic.

'Please, what?' she questioned, because this word she *did* understand.

His black eyes were so cold as they flickered over her face that she wondered if this could really be the same man who had just been kissing her so passionately.

'Spare me the morality lecture, Mia,' he continued. 'You wanted it. I wanted it. It was a mistake. So what?'

She bristled at the way he said it—as if it had been an insignificant event, best forgotten—but at least it sent out a warning that she couldn't afford to be vulnerable around him. Clearing her throat, she attempted to replicate his own cool tone. 'I didn't come here to reignite our physical relationship.'

'I believe you. Believe me, it wasn't what I intended either.' He lowered his voice. 'But the fact that we still want each other throws up something of a dilemma.'

'What sort of dilemma?' she echoed cautiously.

'I suppose the question is, what are we going to do about the insane chemistry which still exists between us?'

Theo's gaze was steady as he registered her look of shock, aware that his words were brutal—but why bother playing games? Why pretend everything was civilised when, beneath the surface, it was anything but? That white-hot desire still burned beneath the surface. It was burning now, despite the coolness of his words. It was making him harder than he could ever remember. How did she *do* that? Was it just the frustration of never having had her, which made him want her so much?

'Because it's a lasting regret of mine,' he continued slowly. 'That I was never *properly* intimate with you.'

'Intimate?' Her shock had given way to surprise and her voice had become very brittle. 'Surely that's nothing but a fancy way of describing sex?'

With a nod of his head, he acknowledged a frankness she would never have used in the past and the baldness of her question should have reassured him she was no longer thinking along foolish fairy-tale lines of love, and romance. But it did no such thing. It didn't reassure him. It made his body tighten and a flare of jealousy begin to ignite. Because underneath it all, Theo was still an old-fashioned man. Especially with her. For this was the woman onto whose finger he had once slid a golden ring, intended to bind them together for life. Where was that ring now? he wondered caustically.

'Perhaps you would prefer me to skip the euphemisms and talk dirty to you,' he suggested silkily. 'Is that what you like these days, Mia? Is that what *turns you on*?'

She tilted her chin—perhaps to conceal the blush he was finding intensely appealing—but all that resulted was that her chestnut ringlets cascaded around her shoulders, and Theo was momentarily transfixed by her voluptuous beauty. Her eyes flashed blue fire and for a moment he thought she was going to rise to his challenge and tell him exactly what she *did* say to the men who had shared her bed. And wouldn't that kill his hunger for her more effectively than anything else, if he imagined her being possessed by another man?

But she said no such thing and he was relieved to have been spared that mental torture.

'How dated your views sound, Theo,' she chided softly. 'What I do in or out of bed is nobody's business but my own. Just like your private life is nothing to do with me. We're divorced in all but name. We've both moved on.'

Had he? Sometimes he wondered. But his track record was irrelevant. There was only one thing which seemed relevant now. His objectives had changed, he realised. They had been changing since he'd sought her out in London. Suddenly it was no longer enough to facilitate a meeting with her grandfather, in order to pay back some of the debt he owed the old man. He had told Mia their kiss had been a mistake, but what if he had been wrong? What if he had been blinding himself to the truth all this time? What if sex with the woman who had deserted him would be less of a complication, and more of a closure?

Because wasn't the reality that Mia had been like a subtle thorn embedded in his flesh all this time? The thorn had burrowed deep enough for him to imagine that it had been absorbed into his body. Determined not to think about her, for the most part he had succeeded—and to the outside world his life was one of supreme accomplishment, on just about every level. No party was ever complete without Theo Aeton on the guest list, with the most glamorous woman in the room hanging eagerly onto his arm. No opening night as special as when the newspapers carried an image of his carved and unsmiling features.

But Mia had always been a shadow lingering on the edges of his heart. She had always represented something unfinished—and for a man whose beginnings had been so messy, that had not sat easily with him. Now he had seen her again. He had touched her and tasted her. Against his will, the fire in his body had been reignited and this time he wanted it to burn out. He wanted more than a kiss and a few frantic stolen caresses. A pulse thudded erratically at his temple. He wanted what should have been his on their wedding night.

Mia.

In his bed.

And him, deep inside her. Doing it to her, over and over again.

Back then she had been a virgin and he would have been the first.

He should have been the first.

But that didn't matter. This wasn't about ego or pride, or his stupidity in putting her on that damned pedestal and essentially placing her out of reach. It was much more fundamental than that. He wanted to have sex with her. To finish off what he had started and erase her from his memory once and for all.

He looked across the room to where she stood, his diminutive copper-headed wife who was surveying him with such belligerent eyes. Yet the desire which shimmered through her delicious body was as palpable as the sunlight which dappled the leaves of the trees outside. It was written in the darkening of her eyes and the trembling of her lips. In the diamond-hard points of her nipples, which were pushing against the cotton of her dress and silently begging for his touch.

Yes, she desired him. Of course she did. He had been desired by women since he'd been barely out of puberty. He gave a bitter smile. How many times had he been told he was irresistible? Or that he resembled a god with his mane of black hair, his glittering ebony eyes and muscle-packed body? But the deep cynicism which ran through Theo's veins made him suspect that his billionaire status might have a lot to do with his allure. Didn't the appeal of diamonds and a bloated bank account exert its own powerful pull on the opposite sex?

Yet Mia had wanted him when he was...

A pulse began to hammer at his temple. Not exactly poor, no—but certainly on a salary which seemed like a drop in the ocean compared to the vast reserves he had now. And wasn't he forgetting something? Yes, she might have professed to have loved him, but those had been meaningless words. How could you tell someone you loved them yet believe they were stealing from you? His throat tightened.

Her words meant nothing.

Love meant nothing.

She had walked away at the first opportunity. His own mother had dumped him, hadn't she? Dumped him and left him to die beside the hulking great ships in the stormy port. Women were capable of cruelty on a grand scale and he should never forget that.

He lifted up his drink, his dust-dry mouth grateful for that first quenching slug of *pressé*, and he put the empty glass down to survey her.

'You say we've moved on but we haven't really, have we, Mia?' he mused. 'Not when we are still man and wife.'

'Only on paper,' she objected.

'But that piece of paper ties us together—
legally at least. And perhaps we need to do something about that.'

A frown pleated her brow. 'Get a…divorce, you
mean?'

'Isn't that what couples usually do when a marriage comes to an end—or fails to start, as in our
case? I thought you were curious to know why I'd
never demanded one before.'

'I was, but if you remember you didn't answer
my question.'

He wanted to hurt her then. To hurt her as she
had hurt him. To make her jealous and realise what
she'd been missing. What she was still missing.
'Some versions of my biography refer to a brief,
early marriage and the assumption is usually made
that the marriage was dissolved.' He smiled. 'And
for a long time, I regarded having a secret wife as
a kind of insurance policy. On one level I enjoyed
keeping the information to myself. Knowing that
no woman had ever become close enough to me
to find out. And of course, it prevented me from
ever doing anything as stupid as getting married
again.' He gave the ghost of a smile. 'But I am no
longer that man and I have no great need to pro-
tect myself.'

'You mean…' Her voice faltered. 'You've found
someone you want to marry? Someone else?'

He saw the distress she was trying to hide—

and he let her endure it for a moment longer before he answered, because he wanted to hurt her as she had hurt him.

'I never say never, but that's unlikely to happen. For me, it's more a question of tying up all the loose ends and simplifying my life. There is nothing to stop us from agreeing a settlement and you could walk away from this marriage as a wealthy woman.' He shrugged. 'Naturally, I would be prepared to be more than...*generous*.'

But he saw no obvious reaction of pleasure or greed. He watched her eyes narrow—as if the idea of walking away with a massive settlement was a burden rather than a liberation.

'If only you knew how patronising you sound!' she declared. 'It makes me realise what a lucky escape I had. I don't *need* your *generosity*—I've managed very well without it so far!'

Her feisty attitude made her even more desirable. The flash of fire which lit up her blue eyes was very beguiling, as was the sudden pout of anger which made him want to crush her soft lips beneath his own. If it had been any other woman than Mia, this conversation would have ended one way only—with them in bed. But it *was* Mia, which made it complicated.

'You think so?' he queried. 'That's surely a matter for debate. You can't tell me you're happy working as a maid and living in cramped accommodation in the city? I always thought you were a country girl, at heart.'

She opened her mouth as if to respond, then seemed to think better of it, drawing her shoulders back in a gesture of kittenish pride. 'When I want any career advice from you, I'll be sure to let you know.'

In spite of himself, he smiled. 'As you wish,' he said softly. 'Now, why don't you settle in while I'm working? Use the pool if you want. There's a library if you want to read. And later, I'll take you to see your grandfather.'

He glanced down at her suitcase, which stood in the middle of the floor, and thought how out of place the battered piece of luggage looked in the pristine surroundings. His mouth hardened. He would facilitate a reconciliation between her and her grandfather, and afterwards, he and Mia could meet with his lawyer and agree a divorce. Then, and only then—when the connection between them had been legally severed—might he consider having sex with her.

He gave a flicker of a smile. When he stopped to think about it, it might be a fitting kind of farewell.

CHAPTER FIVE

AFTER THEO HAD GONE, Mia realised she was shaking. Actually *shaking*. Was that down to the sensual encounter she'd ended so abruptly, or the difficult conversation which had followed on from that? She fished around in her handbag for her hairbrush. It didn't matter. None of that mattered.

She went into the en-suite bathroom adjoining her bedroom—which was even bigger than the bathroom in the Presidential Suite of the Granchester hotel, which was saying something. All gleaming marble and silvery fittings, it contained a bath the size of a small swimming pool, a rainfall shower—and as many luxurious scented creams and gels as you'd find in an upmarket department store.

But all this unashamed opulence left Mia cold as she washed her hands and splashed water onto her face, though it had little effect on the vivid flush of her complexion. All she could think about was Theo and what he'd done when he'd pulled her into his arms and started to kiss her. Or rather, what he *hadn't* done. Because she'd been up for it, hadn't she? Deep down, she had been longing for him to sweep her into his arms and carry her over to that huge bed and do what she had been aching for him to do for so long now.

Why *hadn't* he?

That was her secret, shameful fantasy. Why hadn't she just encouraged him and gone for it? she thought crossly. Surely it would have freed them both from this niggling frustration which seemed to have been reactivated without either of them wanting it to.

She stared into the mirror, at the natural blue shade of her eyes, which was almost obscured by the blackness of her pupils. Her mind was buzzing as she dried her fingers on a fluffy towel and began to indulge in forbidden thoughts. What would sex with Theo be like? she wondered. What if, after all these years of longing and regret, it turned out to be a big fat disappointment? Would that be ironic, or disappointing? Liberating, even? She sighed. No. She mustn't lose sight of reality. How could sex with Theo Aeton be anything other than blissful?

But that wasn't why she was here. She was here to build bridges and be a dutiful granddaughter to a man who needed her and who now, it seemed, was regretting having rejected her.

Quickly, she unpacked the contents of her suitcase, thinking how forlorn her cheap clothes looked hanging in a tiny segment of the bank of fitted wardrobes. She finished off her lemon drink and tried to read a book about canine infectious diseases, but the words were nothing but a blur on the page because Theo's darkly golden looks kept flitting distractingly into her mind.

Putting the book down, she glanced at her watch. There were still a couple of hours to go until they left to see Pappous and if she had to stay in this room much longer, she'd go nuts. She found the swimming costume she'd brought and hauled it on over her protesting curves, before pulling on an all-concealing wrap. Mia wasn't as insecure about her body as she used to be and the world was a lot more accepting of different shapes these days, but even so, she still didn't relish looking at herself in a full-length mirror.

Slipping through the marble corridors, she made her way to the pool, where the cool water felt like liquid silk gliding over her heated flesh as she slipped beneath the surface. Purposefully, she swam length after length until she was pleasantly tired and finished up in the infinity section, where she floated on her back and tried to enjoy the bright Greek sunshine and the tantalising scent of lemon and pine which drifted through the air.

After a while she headed back to her room, dived into the rainfall shower and, after a bit of indecision about which of her three dresses she should wear, presented herself downstairs at the appointed hour, to find Theo waiting for her.

His powerful figure dominated the airy entrance hall and her already thudding heart missed a beat. His eyes were shielded by a pair of dark glasses which made him resemble an enigmatic movie star and he was wearing a cool grey suit which emphasised his towering height. Silently, Mia acknowledged the sting of her breasts. He looked tantalising yet somehow unapproachable— and everyone knew that things which were out of reach were always more alluring than things which were there for the taking. At least, that's what she tried to tell herself.

And anyway, Theo's allure was not her primary concern—and neither was the smoulder of heat which had begun to whisper over her skin. A very important meeting lay ahead and she could tell from the clamminess of her palms just how nervous she really was.

'Ready?' he questioned.

'I'm scared,' she admitted.

'Don't be.' The curve of his lips was almost kind. 'You're his favourite granddaughter.'

'I'm his only granddaughter,' she retorted as she stepped into the afternoon sunshine to see a gleaming black car sitting outside. 'Where's the chauffeur?' she questioned, peering inside.

'No chauffeur. I'm driving.'

'Really?'

'Does that bother you?'

'Why should it?' she answered insouciantly, sliding into the passenger seat and smoothing down the skirt of her cotton dress. 'You may have many faults, Theo—but as I recall, poor driving wasn't one of them.'

Theo bit back a smile as he removed his jacket before getting behind the wheel, aware of the subtle scent of shampoo and soap which was radiating from his passenger and somehow the innocent freshness of those combined fragrances seemed disproportionately evocative. It made him feel uncomfortable. It reminded him of the man he had once been, and the man he was today. But that earlier version of himself had been a fool. He had mistaken desire for emotion. He had been taken hostage by his own feelings and had vowed never to let that happen again.

For a while he said nothing as he drove towards the old man's house, but when he could resist no longer, he shot her a glance, noting the tense way she was sitting. 'How was your afternoon?'

'It was all right. I went swimming.'

'I saw.'

She turned her head, with a cascade of bright curls. 'You were watching me?'

'Didn't you catch the glint of my binoculars in the sunshine?'

'You *are* kidding?'

He heard the squeak of horror in her voice and a smile played at the edges of his lips. 'Don't worry, Mia. I've never had to resort to voyeurism,' he informed her drily. 'I happened to look out of the window and saw you dive in.'

'It was an awful dive.'

'It could have been better,' he agreed. 'You should have kept your head down.'

'I wasn't actually asking for your advice.'

Theo decreased his speed and turned off down a smaller road leading towards the sea, his hands gripping the wheel tightly. He was behaving as if her technique had been his key consideration, when that had been the last thing on his mind. He had seen her splash into the water and had quickly moved away from the window because gazing at his half-naked wife had been doing dangerous things to his blood pressure.

But he hadn't been able to get the image of a swimsuit-clad Mia out of his head. It had made his body clench with hunger as he had stared blankly at his computer screen, the complicated sequence of numbers making little sense. The only thing he could see was a green swimsuit clinging to the curves of her body and dark red spirals of her hair contrasting against the glimmering blue of the water. It had taken every ounce of his resolve to resist the temptation to set aside his work and go and join her in the pool.

'We're here,' he said as they drove in through the big wooden gates of her grandfather's estate.

'I can see that for myself. I have been here before, Theo. Remember?'

Her words were spiky, but couldn't disguise the unmistakable nervousness underpinning them, and although vulnerability was a characteristic he tended to avoid, for once Theo was curious. As they reached the front of the house, he cut the engine and turned to look at her, observing the strained set of her profile as she gazed straight ahead. 'How does it feel, being back here?'

He expected her to cut off his question with an impatient aside or to tell him that was also none of his business. But to his surprise, she didn't. She spoke as if he weren't there. As if she had forgotten who he was, or where she was. 'How do you think it feels? It's…painful. It brings back memories I'd rather not have. It still hurts that he rejected me for all those years and made me vow never to set foot on his land again.' She bit her lip. 'But things change. I'm happy he's asked to see me again. If he hadn't… Well, I don't think I would ever have returned, to be honest.'

Theo felt the stab of something uncomfortable as he got out of the car, intending to open her door but Mia had already jumped out. She was standing in the sunshine, looking up at the big white house with a wistful expression on her face, the flower-sprigged dress making her look so unbelievably pretty that for a moment he couldn't drag his eyes away.

He had always come and gone as he pleased on the sprawling property and today that suited his purpose. It meant he could avoid bumping into any of the servants, because he was in no mood for conversation. He could see Mia's gaze darting here and there—as if registering what was the same and what was different. And her sudden look of sadness produced in him a powerful stir of guilt.

'Would you like to walk around first?' he questioned abruptly. 'Maybe acclimatise yourself with the place before you go in?'

She nodded. 'Yes. I'd like that.'

In contemplative silence, Mia fell into step beside him as they began to walk through the extensive grounds, along shaded paths lined with large pots of neglected plants and unpruned orange trees. She started wondering if Theo was thinking along the same lines as her. Was he looking at the outdated rectangular swimming pool and remembering the way the two of them had dived and raced like fishes, their laughter pealing through the sultry heat of the Greek air? But now the pool looked forgotten, with fallen leaves floating forlornly on the surface.

'Does nobody come here any more?' she asked suddenly.

Theo shook his dark head. 'Only me,' he said.

Mia felt a stab of guilt. Theo wasn't even a blood relation. She was, yet she'd stayed away all these years. She felt as if she'd had a raw deal with her family—as if she'd been short-changed on just about every level—and her grandfather's snub had been the final nail in the coffin. But maybe she hadn't been looking at the bigger picture.

Had she allowed her pride and hurt to keep her away from a place which had felt like the closest thing she'd ever had to home? She had been scared her grandfather might reject her, yes—but she had been just as scared of bumping into Theo. Had she subconsciously realised that his effect on her would be as powerful as it had always been, no matter how many years had passed—and wasn't there something awfully sad about that? It was a myth that she had distanced herself from her husband and he no longer had any influence on her life. Behind the scenes it seemed he had never really stopped influencing her.

'I'd like to go and see Pappous now,' she said.

He nodded and they reversed their steps through the unkempt gardens to make their way towards the house, until they came to a halt in front of some shuttered doors on the ground floor.

'Are you ready?' he questioned, pushing open one of the doors. 'You'd better prepare yourself, Mia,' he added softly. 'He isn't the man he once was.'

There was a moment of hesitation, before she nodded. 'I'm ready.'

No sound came from within and the silence felt immense as they stepped into the dimly lit room, where the air was cool and air-conditioned. A nurse dressed all in white sat motionless beside the bed and, catching sight of Theo, she nodded and rose noiselessly from her chair, before slipping from the room.

With a fierce knotting of her heart, Mia looked around, her gaze taking in all the paraphernalia of end-of-life care. The neatly lined bottles of tablets. The sterile dressing pack. A jug of water covered with an embroidered cloth and the glass beside it, the liquid untouched. The figure in the bed was covered with a sheet and completely inert but even from here she could see how much his once mighty frame had diminished. She gave a little snuffle. She wondered if it was that which made Theo reach out to touch her elbow. It was the lightest contact imaginable—yet wasn't it crazy how that

simple gesture could feel so warm and comforting?
As if he were her rock and she could lean on him.
Was her grandfather sleeping? she wondered. Or
was it wishful thinking which made her imagine
a faint flickering movement of his eyelids?

But before she had a chance to investigate a
bundle of brown and white fur came hurtling
across the room towards her, yapping and jumping
up excitedly, its paws scrabbling wildly at Mia's
dress as the animal began to yelp with joy and
confusion.

'Tycheros!' Mia whispered in disbelief, strok-
ing his head and blinking back her tears as she
crouched down and stared into the face of the dog
she had rescued as a puppy. Instantly, the animal
rolled onto its back, paws in the air as it bared
its pink belly in a gesture of total trust and submission. 'Oh, Tycheros,' she said again, her voice
catching as she whispered half to herself, 'I never
thought I'd see you again.'

'Mia?' An unsteady rasp rattled from the direction of the bed and there was a sudden rustling of
the sheet. 'Mia? Is that you?'

She could see now that her grandfather's ancient
eyes were definitely glittering but Tycheros was
still barking and it sounded unrealistically loud
in the subdued atmosphere of the sickroom. Mia
tried to quieten him with a cautionary forefinger
but the dog Theo had christened Lucky continued

to jump up with whines of delight, its tail waving back and forth like the windscreen wiper on a car. 'Will you take him outside?' she asked Theo firmly and as he led the dog away, she walked slowly towards the bed. '*Ochi*, Pappous. It's me. It's Mia. Oh, Pappous!'

With great difficulty—and waving away her offer of help—the figure in the bed wriggled up to get a better look and it took all the fortitude she possessed not to recoil in shock when she saw the pain-filled face of her grandfather. Because Theo had been right—it *was* a shock to see him like this.

Georgios Minotis had always been so robust and strong—a powerhouse of a man who had seemed to defy the years. Last time she'd seen him he had been full of life and vigour. But now? She blinked. Now he was nothing but a husk—a mere shadow of his former self. The salty spring of tears gathered in her eyes as she thought of all the time she had wasted. All those years they would never get back. Why hadn't she just taken the initiative and come here before? Swallowed her stupid pride before he did, and made amends?

'I should have known it,' Georgios snapped, his hooded gaze flickering towards the window where Tycheros was now pursuing a stick which Theo had presumably hurled towards the far end of the garden. 'Damned animal growls at anyone else. Even Theo.'

'Oh, Pappous,' Mia whispered, preparing to go over and hug him tightly, with all the love which was bubbling up inside her, even as she acknowledged that illness seemed to have done little to subdue his famously cranky nature.

But there was no answering softness in the faded black eyes as they turned to scrutinise her. They were filled with an emotion Mia didn't recognise. Or maybe she just couldn't bear to.

'What the hell are *you* doing here?' he demanded.

She tried to tell herself that sickness made people volatile and not to react to the hostility which was etched on his face, but it was difficult not to be hurt by his callous greeting. 'I'm here to see you, Pappous,' she offered cautiously.

'Why? Who let you in? Who brought you here?'

Mia hadn't even noticed him return from the garden but Theo must have been standing in the shadows at the edge of the room. He stepped forward, his powerful body seeming to fill the place with purpose.

'I did,' he said. 'I brought her.'

'Why the hell did you do that?' Spidery venom distorted the old man's voice and the lines on his ravaged face became even more pronounced. 'I told you I never wanted to see her again.'

'Because I thought you should see her,' said Theo calmly. 'That it would be good for you.'

'What right do you have to know what is *good* for me?' The old man's gaze raked over Mia, his voice quavering as he sneered. 'What do you want? My money? Has your mother sent you to claw back what you can from a dying man?'

'No,' said Mia, the hurt she felt at being spoken to that way now morphing into a slow and simmering anger. Briefly, she glared at Theo, before once more meeting her grandfather's eyes. 'My mother lives in Florida now. I may not see her very often but she certainly doesn't want your money. Your tainted money!' she added, wondering if she had imagined the brief nod of acknowledgement from her grandfather, as if he were only capable of dealing with people who dared stand up to him.

Had she been naïve enough to think he'd changed? That he had undergone a sudden transformation which had freed him from the shackles of his mistrustful mind, which made him unable to look at anyone without suspecting they were after his money? Well, she wasn't going to stay here and listen to it. She had escaped from the cesspit of this toxic world and she had no intention of jumping straight back into it.

She was about to head back towards the garden when Theo stayed her with the faintest shake of his head before beginning to speak, the resonance of his words whispering over her skin like velvet, as he captured her in his night-dark gaze. 'You might change your mind about that, Georgios. When you hear what we're about to tell you.'

Mia's anger was superseded by confusion as she looked from Theo to her grandfather. *We?* What was he talking about? Why was he making it sound as if they were a unit? A couple—instead of two people on the brink of divorce. And why *had* he brought her here when clearly she wasn't wanted? He must have known that. Maybe he hadn't thought or cared that this kind of reception could hurt. Or maybe he thought she deserved to be hurt.

But she could see that her grandfather's face had changed. The hostility had vanished and he was looking at the two of them with interest. As if the world had very few surprises left for him and he was curious to hear what Theo had to say. Come to think of it, she was pretty curious herself.

And then everything began to change in a way she could never have imagined. Theo's arm was snaking around her waist with a familiarity which felt sublimely comfortable as well as very sexy. Suddenly their bodies were touching, and she cursed the appreciative shiver she gave as her fleshy hip collided with the bony jut of his.

'Can't you guess?' he said softly. 'We're back together. Mia and Theo. Husband and wife.'

He dropped a soft kiss on top of Mia's head and she cursed him for that too because, despite all her best intentions, it was making her long for things she had no right to long for.

It was all an act, she reminded herself bitterly. Nothing but an act. Just as it always had been.

She knew she ought to tear herself away, but Mia didn't move. She told herself it was because any protest she made would appear callous—especially when her grandfather's wide smile seemed to have taken ten years off him. As she registered the delight which had transformed the old man into a closer approximation of the person he had once been, she felt trapped and compromised—but, in a strange way, willingly so. A feeling which was intensified by Tycheros, who must have slunk back into the room unnoticed and was quietly licking her hand. That crazy feeling of coming home assaulted her yet again, and the weakening effect of Theo's touch was making her powerless to resist.

'You are intending to make this marriage work?' the old man verified querulously.

'We certainly are,' affirmed Theo, a silky emphasis in his voice as he stroked his thumb over the base of her spine.

Mia looked up into his face to silently warn him to stop all this playacting, but his black eyes were glittering with something she didn't recognise. As he tilted her chin and bent his head towards her, she realised with a mixture of horror and delight that Theo Aeton was about to kiss her.

It was a show put on solely for the benefit of a captive audience. And even though his lips conveyed no other emotion than the hard stamp of possession, it didn't stop Mia from closing her eyes and kissing him back.

CHAPTER SIX

'I CAN'T *BELIEVE* you just did that!' Mia howled, as the car purred back through the gates of her grand-father's estate. Furiously, she turned to stare at Theo's profile, irritated beyond measure that the accusations she'd been hurling at him since they'd left the house didn't seem to be hitting home, be-cause his features remained as implacable as ever, his gaze fixed responsibly on the road in front of him. 'Or maybe I can believe it. You've got form for being sneaky and underhand, haven't you, Theo?'

'Will you please calm down?'

'No, I will not. Don't keep telling me to calm down, as if you're working on some telephone helpline.'

'I realise you're angry.'

'Too damned right, I'm angry.' Mia bit into a lip which, infuriatingly, kept wobbling. 'In fact, I can never remember feeling this furious.'

Or betrayed. That was the worst bit. Once again, Theo had betrayed her by doing something which impacted deeply on her life, without any prior consultation. Yes, he might have brought delight to a dying man—but he had done so by placing her in an invidious position. And she couldn't see how she was going to get out of it.

Yet hadn't she betrayed *herself*—and in front of them all? Theo, her grandfather, and the one-eyed dog she'd found bleeding on the roadside all those years ago and which Theo had christened Lucky—saying how lucky the animal had been to have been rescued by her.

Mia huffed out another angry breath. When her estranged husband had pulled her into his arms and branded her lips with a fiery kiss intended for show hadn't she responded as if he had just made the most romantic gesture in the world? She had practically swooned as his mouth had covered hers and she'd kissed him back with a hunger which had been building inside her all day. She'd heard the grunt of approval her grandfather had given—as if they had just demonstrated to his satisfaction that a reconciliation was definitely on the cards. They had pulled apart and for a moment she had just stood there, grinning stupidly, her face flushed with pleasure as Theo's fingers curved possessively around her hip.

Had she learned *nothing*? Was she still that

same woman so desperate for this man that she
would accept whatever scraps he deigned to throw
her way?

'When you touched my arm when we first went
in, was that touching little squeeze of comfort just
for show too?' she demanded. 'Did you do it because you knew my grandfather was watching and
would falsely interpret it as a sign of true affection?'

He flicked her a brief look. 'You really think
I'm that calculating?'

'I don't think it, Theo. I know it.'

His eyes returned to the road ahead. 'Very well,
Mia. Think the worst about me, if you must. You
think I care?'

His arrogant query only increased her fury but
Mia didn't say another word for the rest of the
drive home. She thought it unwise to give vent to
her rage while he was driving and Theo seemed
content to let her fume in silence. When he stopped
the car in front of the house she went straight out
into the garden to try to cool off, strangely confident he would follow her—which he did. And
though she didn't *want* to feel a spear of sexual
excitement, she wasn't going to deny the thrill it
gave her to know that this devastatingly handsome
man was pursuing her through the grounds of his
property. Was that because, for the first time in

their relationship, she felt as if *she* was the one
with the power?

Her mind had been whirling with possibilities
about where to have this very necessary confron-
tation. She didn't want to go to the bedroom and
she certainly wasn't going to talk to him in the
house, with Sofia and his maid hovering in the
background. She didn't want to be overheard, or
disturbed.

Her footsteps were fast and so was the beat of
her heart, but it was difficult to maintain a high
level of outrage when everything looked so beautiful in the honeyed light of the setting sun. The
approach of evening had made the perfume of the
flowers even more pronounced, and the wide rib-
bon of sea looked as if it had been highlighted
with strokes of glittering bronze. A sudden sense
of melancholy cloaked her, as she acknowledged
the beauty all around her. Why couldn't she just
sit down and enjoy the glory of her surroundings,
as she used to do in the old days when she used to
come to Greece during her summer holidays? Because everything had changed, that was why. For a
start, she wasn't on holiday. She was here on suf-
ferance and Theo had lied to her. Those were the
facts. Stark and unpalatable, but true. Again, she
felt the wash of anger, but Mia waited until they
were alone in a courtyard garden she'd noticed on
her way back from the pool, as she steadied her

breath for long enough to ensure that her words were coherent.

'Why did you spring that on me, Theo?' she demanded. 'My grandfather didn't even know I was coming, did he? I couldn't believe it when I walked in and saw the shock and, yes, the horror on his face. I felt like I'd ambushed him, or something. Which I suppose, in a way, I had.' She shook her head and felt the tickle of wayward curls brushing against her warm skin. 'He hadn't expressed any desire for some sort of reconciliation with me, had he? There was to be no touching deathbed conversion.'

There was silence.

'Have you finished?' he questioned quietly.

'No, I haven't finished! I haven't even started, to be honest, except you probably wouldn't recognise honesty if it came up and hit you in the face.' She sucked in a shaky breath and suddenly she was afraid of doing something irreversible—like bursting into tears of disappointment and making him realise he still had the power to hurt her. Even now. 'You told me a big fat lie, Theo,' she whispered. 'You brought me out here under false pretences and what I want to know is…why? I mean, what's in it for you?'

'You think that's my only motivation?' His eyes narrowed. 'Self-interest?'

'I do, yes. Leopards don't change their spots.'

Oddly frustrated by her negative assessment of him, Theo turned to look at a statue of a woman, into whose marble basket one of the gardeners must have placed a bright, pink bloom which was glowing in the fading light. Suddenly, a bird flew on top of the statue's head and began to sing its heart out, and as the sweet notes penetrated his consciousness he felt as if he had just woken up from a long sleep.

When was the last time he had been in this part of the garden? he wondered, enjoying the violet and rose light which illuminated his surroundings and which made him feel as if he were standing in the middle of an oil painting. He frowned. He never really came here to enjoy the beauty or stop to reflect, did he? Just as he never used his pool for anything other than relentless, early-morning exercise. He had always been so driven. So determined never to take his foot off the accelerator. He had never really learned how to relax, or to enjoy the moment. He wondered what had made him think of that now.

Dragging his thoughts away from unwelcome reflection, he stared into the accusatory glitter of Mia's blue eyes. 'You want to hear my side of the story?'

She pursed her lips together before nodding, pushing away the tangle of her copper curls. 'It would be a start,' she conceded grudgingly.

He wished she wouldn't do that with her lips because it made it difficult not to start thinking about kissing her again. Theo cleared his throat. 'Let's start with the land. I have no self-interest— certainly not of the monetary kind. I never have. The piece of coastline your father gifted to me on our wedding day is in your name. I signed it over to you the day after your somewhat...' his mouth twisted mockingly '...abrupt departure.'

'You mean...' She stared at him. 'It's been mine all the time?'

'Yes.'

'But you didn't bother telling me?'

'Why should I?' He gave a sardonic laugh. 'You expected me to go chasing after you, did you, Mia? Pleading with you for your forgiveness? I thought you would return and when you didn't...' He shrugged, making out he hadn't cared, when at the time he had. More than he'd thought possible. Yet her sustained absence had worked in his favour, or so he'd thought. He'd convinced himself she was nothing but a child—too scared to come back and face the music—and that he'd had a lucky escape. He felt as if her response had given him permission to go out and behave as he wanted to behave. Which he had done.

'I felt pretty sure you wouldn't come back if you thought the old man was going to reject you,' he continued, fixing her with a piercing look. 'Am I right?'

'I suppose so,' she said reluctantly.

'And yes, your grandfather can be an annoying and cantankerous old man,' he said slowly. 'But I have never forgotten the way he helped me, when I had nothing. I wanted to help him, and the bottom line is that he always wanted us to stay together, as man and wife. For some reason, he imagined we shared something which could work.' He held his hand up, his lips hardening into a stony slash. 'It's okay. You don't have to tell me you don't share his opinion—I can read it on your face. For what it's worth, I happen to agree with you.'

'You do?' she questioned.

'Of course I do. Our marriage was a mistake. It should never have happened. You were too young and I was determined to do the right thing, because I knew how much it would hurt him if I simply had an affair with you. So I asked you to marry me.'

'Right,' she said, trying to tell herself that here at least she could silently commend him for his honesty, but stupidly enough—it hurt. 'That's the reason you wanted me to be your wife? You didn't want to take my virginity without putting a ring on my finger, just to please your great mentor?'

'What's the point in raking over all that now?' he questioned impatiently. 'The past is just the past and the point is that he's dying, Mia. We can both see that. And his greatest wish was—is—for us to stay married.' He paused, his eyes narrowing as he met the stubborn expression on her face. 'Couldn't we give him what he wants—if only for a short while?'

'What good will that do?' she answered sulkily.

'We could make an old man happy enough to reconcile with the granddaughter he loves and free you both from the chains of bitterness,' he said roughly. 'Don't you want that to happen? Or will you go away from here with his angry words ringing in your ears, and live to regret the fact that he died without the two of you having made up?'

'Don't you dare play with my emotions!' she howled.

'I'm not playing with your emotions. I'm trying to use my own experience to prevent you from doing something which can never be undone.'

'What experience?' she questioned, her blue eyes suddenly growing hooded.

Theo delayed answering because this was a subject he never addressed. Not with her. Not with anyone. Why probe a sore which would be better left to heal on its own? Or shine a light on the shadows of his past and make him aware of just how grim that past had been?

But perhaps some sort of explanation was necessary—more as a bargaining tool than for any real desire for her to learn more about him, because it was too late for that now. Already she knew more than most people, yet she still thought the worst of him in any situation. But she didn't know this bit. Nobody did. He had seen to that. Early on in his career, he had taken control of all available information about himself and deliberately sanitised his background. He had shaved away the facts until they were nothing but dull bullet points. Little of his life before Georgios Minotis had adopted him was known, except perhaps to this woman with the wary blue eyes.

'My mother dumped me as a baby,' he said harshly.

'Yes.' Her voice had softened now with husky affirmation. 'I know that, Theo.'

And she had never talked about it, he realised suddenly. She might have used her knowledge as a weapon against him when she'd discovered that her grandfather had given him the land. Yet, despite her pain, she hadn't brought those juicy facts into the public arena and capitalised on what she knew—she had stayed loyal to him. Other women in her situation might have been tempted to sell their story, but Mia hadn't chosen that route. She had preferred to live in humble obscurity in London, rather than rake in the money she could have earned from some downmarket tabloid with an appetite for the secret lives of billionaires.

His jaw clenched, because this wasn't supposed

to be about concentrating on her good traits. It was all about winning her over to his idea. His mouth hardened. 'Over the years, I've read enough literature to understand that such an abandonment can have a profound effect on the psyche of the child—'

'How forensic you sound,' she breathed.

He slanted her a cool and questioning look. Would she have preferred to see him go to pieces? To demonstrate the kind of frailties which might make him appear weak? Then she would be waiting a long time, he concluded grimly. He thought back to when she had run away and the bitter tang of emptiness he had experienced as a result. He had hated feeling that way—that sense of emotional dependence he'd never fallen victim to before or since. Was that why he had decided to discover more about his roots—as a way of distracting himself? As a way of getting Mia Minotis off his mind?

'After the debacle of our wedding, I decided to seek out my mother,' he told her. 'To discover what circumstances had forced her to take such a desperate step.' He could feel the rough catch at the back of his throat and wondered how, even after all this time, it still had the power to affect him. 'I thought she must have been destitute. That perhaps she still was, and that maybe I ought to help her, as I had become a wealthy man. And don't they say that altruism always makes a person feel better about themselves?' he enquired mockingly.

'I guess they do,' came her response, toneless enough to barely register in his troubled thoughts.

'But it seemed any altruism on my part was unnecessary,' he continued, and a pulse began to thud angrily at his temple. 'I discovered that my mother had married, and married well. She was an extremely wealthy woman herself, though childless. Maybe she never liked children.' His lips curved with derision. 'Why else would she have chosen to abandon a helpless infant in a torrential dockside gutter, where they were most likely never to have been discovered?'

There was silence for a moment as she absorbed this. 'Oh, Theo,' she said at last, but must have noticed his gaze warning her against sympathy, for she quickly changed tack. 'You must have been so angry.'

He nodded. Angry, yes—but surprised, too. And the biggest surprise had been in finding out how much it had hurt. Like every child, Theo had painted vivid pictures in his imagination. He had imagined his mother as young and frightened and abandoned. A distraught woman at the end of her tether, who could see no way out other than to abandon her beloved child. What he had not expected was to find a face-lifted socialite, sipping cocktails on a vulgar yacht. With a little digging, he had discovered there had been a period of absence in the recorded story of her life. A year's absence, to be precise. Long enough for her to have a secret baby and then to leave it on the ground, like a piece of rubbish.

'So what did you do?' she probed, her blue eyes wide and troubled. 'Did you get in touch with her?'

'Of course I didn't,' he negated. 'Why would I? The thought of even being in the same room as her made my flesh crawl. So I left her to her privileged life and carried on with my own.' He sucked in a deep breath and slowly let it out. 'Until one day I received word that she had died and I...'

'What, Theo?' she prompted as his words tailed off. 'How did that make you feel?'

This was the kind of intrusive query women often liked to make, but when Mia asked it—with her voice so soft and concerned—Theo found himself answering, almost without meaning to. But he didn't give her the uncensored version, because that would be a confidence too far. He didn't tell her that he'd wanted to throw his head back and howl with rage and bewilderment.

'I found myself regretting not asking her why she'd done it,' he admitted. 'Why she had made such a cruel and potentially dangerous decision. And I realised that now I would never get the chance. Because death really is final, Mia.' His gaze bored into her. 'Intellectually, it's something

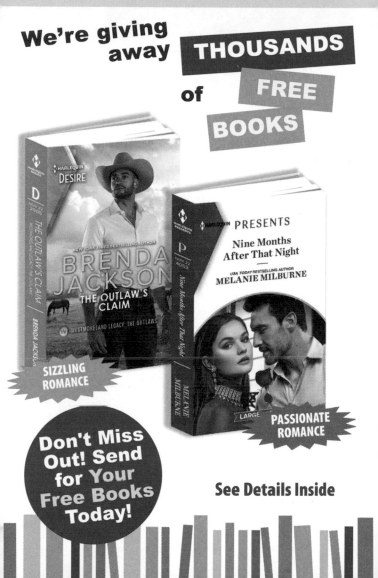

Get up to 4
FREE FABULOUS BOOKS
You Love!

To thank you for being a loyal reader we'd like to send you up to 4 FREE BOOKS, absolutely free when you try the Harlequin Reader Service.

Just write "YES" on the Loyal Reader Voucher and we'll send you 2 free books from each series you choose and Free Mystery Gifts, altogether worth over $20.

Try **Harlequin® Desire** and get 2 books featuring the worlds of the American elite with juicy plot twists, delicious sensuality and intriguing scandal.

Try **Harlequin Presents® Larger-Print** and get 2 books featuring the glamourous lives of royals and billionaires in a world of exotic locations, where passion knows no bounds.

Or **TRY BOTH and get 2 books from each series!**

Your free books are completely free, even the shipping! If you continue with your subscription, you can look forward to curated monthly shipments of brand-new books from your selected series, always at a discount off the cover price! Plus you can cancel any time.

So don't miss out, return your Loyal Readers Voucher today to get your Free books.

Pam Powers

LOYAL READER
FREE BOOKS VOUCHER

we all know—but somehow we never really believe it's true. I think you'll regret not making up with the old man, no matter how much you try to convince yourself otherwise.'

The concern had left her eyes and in its place was the blue spark of mutiny. 'And presumably you've told me all this to guilt-trip me into agreeing to your ridiculous scheme?'

'Is it really such a ridiculous scheme?' he questioned curiously.

'You know it is.'

'Why? I think we could convince the world we're a reconciled couple, don't you? You don't seem to have any problems responding to me as a loving wife might do,' he continued, and now his mind was filled with a whisper of erotic possibility. 'Not earlier and not at your grandfather's, when I kissed you,' he concluded huskily.

'I expect most women react like that when you kiss them?'

'And if they do?' he drawled.

He saw her wince.

'It doesn't matter,' she said quickly, the flush in her cheeks intensifying. 'So it won't actually mean anything—this marriage of ours?'

'How *can* it mean anything? It will be a fake marriage. A marriage of convenience. And would it really be so different from a million others?'

She pushed a bright curl away from where it had strayed to the edge of her mouth. 'What others?'

Theo could feel the sudden powering of his heart because all he could think about was covering that mouth with his. Or feeling her lips at his groin, circling the stiff shaft which was currently throbbing with frustration and need. 'I'm talking about unhappy couples, and unhappy marriages. I know plenty of those, don't you, Mia? I have no illusions about the institution of marriage. But all the people who are unhappy don't automatically separate. Some of them stay together for years. Some for all of their lives. They hide their pain and their boredom and their infidelities behind different masks.' He ground out a bitter laugh. 'So why don't we find our own masks to wear? Why don't we remind the world that we are man and wife, for your grandfather's sake?' His ebony eyes glittered. 'It's not for ever. At most, a few months. And afterwards, we can divorce.'

'Are you…serious?'

'Why wouldn't I be?'

'There's my job, for a start. I arranged three weeks' leave of absence—this could be a much longer arrangement.'

He shrugged. 'You're a maid, and maids are easily replaceable.'

'Not good ones,' she argued hotly. 'And besides, I got promoted. I became a housekeeper, and then a supervisor, which is what I'm doing at the moment, though not for much longer.'

His eyes narrowed. 'Why, what else are you planning?'

Mia twiddled a coppery curl with her finger as she gazed up into his face, because suddenly it became important for her to make him understand that she hadn't just stayed static since they'd been apart. That the person he'd judged her to be wasn't the person she really was.

'I realised I didn't want to stay working in a city hotel,' she said, her attention momentarily caught by a pale moth fluttering frantically in the dying light of the day. 'You probably don't remember, but my dream had always been to work with animals.'

'The first time I met you, you were holding Tycheros,' he said slowly.

Mia blinked. 'You remember that?'

'How could I forget?' A look of something vaguely uncomfortable passed across his features. 'You were covered in his blood from where that bastard had taken out his eye with an air gun, but you didn't flinch. I'd never seen a woman behave like that before.' He shook his head. 'With such courage and such fortitude.'

Something about his approval made her go all mushy inside and her needy response angered her. Mia forced herself to concentrate on the facts because even *feeling* this vulnerable was dangerous, let alone showing it. It suited her much better to think he'd married her to get his hands on the land—only now she'd discovered that he hadn't done that either.

'I've been saving up to go to school to be a veterinary nurse,' she continued. 'I've got a place which starts in September and in the meantime I help at the dog rescue centre in my spare time. So I can't just come and live here indefinitely in what sounds like a horrendous situation. *Pretending to be your wife!*' She shook her head. 'I've forged a new life for myself and it's one I'm proud of.'

But his expression remained implacable.

'You've seen how sick he is,' he said. 'The doctors told me it would be a matter of weeks. It's now April, and your college place doesn't start until September.' He paused. 'What if we see how things go? I can always get my team to help the Granchester find a replacement for you, if needed, so you're not leaving them in the lurch. Couldn't you do it? For him?'

Mia hesitated. The obvious answer was no, especially when she considered the pain she could inflict on herself by agreeing to such a crazy masquerade. She wanted to ask whether he'd thought about *her* feelings—or did he just consider them necessary collateral? But if she admitted her worries and her fears wouldn't that make her appear weak? As if she hadn't moved on at all, when clearly he had.

Because earlier today Mia had broken her self-imposed rule of not probing into Theo's life. When she'd got back from her swim and had been killing time, she had given into temptation and looked him up on the Internet. Not the business side of his life, which extolled all his achievements as well as his many virtues, but the other side of his life.

His personal side.

And his vices.

It had been something she had long suspected but finding out for certain had been a chilling wake-up call. Because while Mia had spent the last six years untouched by another man's hand, it seemed Theo had been behaving very differently. With masochistic intent, she had studied the images which had flashed up on her computer while her heart had beaten painfully fast. She'd wanted to shut the screen down but there had been a terrible, irresistible compulsion to keep scrolling down over the photos. And there they were. Paparazzi shots of him with models and actresses. Heiresses and athletes. All of them beautiful. All of them gazing up at him as if they couldn't believe their luck.

Blondes.

Brunettes.

Though interestingly, no redheads.

Why had it hurt so much after all this time to realise he must have had lovers? When she stopped to think about it—why wouldn't he? Unless she was daft enough to think that a rampantly alpha man like Theo would have behaved like a saint after his chubby bride had rejected him.

She had lulled herself into believing that she'd moved on with her promotion and her plans for the future. She'd convinced herself that she didn't care what Theo did or didn't do with his life. But she hadn't moved on at all. Emotionally she had remained stuck in the past—and how was that going to change unless she did something about it? Mia shuddered as she caught a glimpse of the future which could be hers if she stayed locked in this weird kind of limbo. Never having a proper relationship because she never let any man close enough to kiss her—let alone have sex with her.

And she knew why.

Theo Aeton had proved an impossible act to follow, because their relationship had never been allowed to play itself out in a normal way. They were married but they'd never had sex. Their entire association had been underpinned by a deep sense of frustration and a lack of fulfilment. She had yearned for him during their engagement and the bitter truth was that she had yearned for him ever since. Hadn't his harshly beautiful face haunted her dreams when she was least expecting it—

usually when she'd been asked on a date by another man? It was as if her subconscious were determined to remind her that she was setting herself up for an evening of disappointment—which inevitably always came true. It was as if her husband had stamped his presence indelibly on her unconscious mind—and now she was worried she would never be free of his memory.

Unless…

Tilting her chin to survey him with a calmness she was far from feeling, she managed to keep her voice steady. 'What kind of marriage did you have in mind, Theo?'

His expression was inexorable. 'There is only one kind I will consider. A proper marriage.'

And in spite of everything, Mia's heart leapt. She looked at him with breathless hope. Did that mean… Was he actually suggesting they start over? Forget the past and do it properly this time? She swallowed. 'A real marriage?' she echoed, wanting—no, needing—clarification.

'Neh.' His black eyes glittered. 'A marriage with sex. Enough sex so that I'll be able to get you out of my head, once and for all.'

The younger Mia would have wept to have heard such a pitiless declaration, but she was older now. Maybe not much wiser, but certainly her vision was no longer distorted by rose-tinted spectacles. Because what if Theo's vision was the right one? She wanted him and he still wanted her, didn't he? That much was plain. A starving person satisfied their hunger by feeding it, didn't they? So it followed that consummating their relationship, instead of *dreaming* about consummating it, would set her free.

Because she needed that. She really did. She needed to be free of him. And this time she would be no pushover. This time she would be his equal.

She held his gaze for a long moment—long enough to see a flicker of doubt enter his eyes—and then she smiled. 'Okay,' she said at last. 'I'll do it.'

He reached out to cup her face in the palm of his hand, his thumb tracing a slow line around the trembling outline of her lips. And that touch was like magic. Like wildfire. She could feel the instant tug of heat and the slug of her pulse. The molten sweetness at her thighs. Did he realise that already she was wet with need? She ached for him. She wanted him to take her now—with an urgency which might quieten some of this heated agitation. But somehow common sense prevailed and she shook her head, even though she could feel the shiver of her body's indignant objection. 'No,' she said and then, with a little more fervour, 'No.'

He stared at her with undisguised disbelief. 'You've changed your mind?'

'No, I haven't changed my mind, but I'm not

doing it here,' she said, pointing to the fiery ball of the sun which was about to disappear into the sea in a blaze of gold and violet. 'I've waited six long years to have sex with you, Theo Aeton, and it's still light.'

'What's that got to do with anything?' he growled.

'We could be seen,' she said in a low voice. 'And I don't want one of your staff finding us.'

'Nobody will see us. The only other person who comes in here is my gardener—who will have knocked off work a couple of hours ago.'

'I'm not remotely interested in hearing the details of your staff rota!' she hissed. 'I'm just telling you that I have no intention of making out in the open air and being discovered.'

'Not a natural risk-taker, then, Mia?' he probed mockingly.

Momentarily wrong-footed, because his question implied a lot more experience than he was about to discover she had, Mia sought refuge in evasion. 'I couldn't possibly say,' she said carelessly.

He scowled at this, raking his long fingers back through the dark mane of his hair. 'Then we'd better go inside and find ourselves a bedroom,' he said roughly. 'Now.'

CHAPTER SEVEN

'CONSIDERING YOU'VE WAITED *"six long years"* for this,' quoted Theo softly as he began to unbutton his shirt, 'you don't look particularly excited.'

Mia opened her mouth to deny his accusation, but how could she when he'd touched on a raw nerve? Though it wasn't a lack of excitement she was feeling. It was a sheer, primitive terror which seemed to have engulfed everything else. Because her scheme appeared to have backfired on her. She had resisted his kiss in the garden, primly insisting on going inside the house to have sex as if she made those kinds of decisions every minute of the day.

She'd been afraid of losing her virginity in a rapid and undignified way, by allowing herself to get carried away. What if she'd ended up leaning against some marble statue, or lying on an uncomfortable garden lounger which might leave unattractive basket-weave patterns on her bottom? She hadn't said a word of this to Theo, of course, citing the fear of discovery as her reason for stalling. She licked her lips. The trouble was that now Theo obviously thought she was experienced, while nothing could be further from the truth.

He had shut the door of his bedroom quietly behind them and, after sliding the final shirt button from its confinement, was surveying her with a slow scrutiny which was making her heart race.

'I suggest we strip off and get straight into bed,' he said.

'S-strip off?' she verified cautiously.

'I don't know how much longer I can bear to prolong the anticipation,' he confessed, his voice low and velvety. 'Once I start kissing you again, I don't know if I can trust myself not to rip that damned dress from your body. Which would be a shame.' His gaze flickered over her cotton-covered curves. 'Because it's such a pretty dress.'

'Okay,' Mia agreed with a nod of her head, aware of the curls tickling her bare shoulders. She kicked off her sandals. 'Why not?'

She swallowed as his shirt fluttered to the ground and he smiled as he met her widening eyes—as if her rapt voyeurism was perfectly normal. Was this what he usually did when he took a woman to bed? she wondered. Did he stand there removing his clothes with that look of lazy provocation glinting from his eyes, while she was expected to do the same?

Yet in a setting which must have seen far more experienced sexual participants than her, she remained as nervous as hell—and her environment wasn't helping. It was a room which was a testament to masculinity and power. There was no softness here. The soaring dimensions and matchless view over the sapphire sea hinted at the wealth of its owner—as did the bold oil paintings, the glass sculpture of a woman, and a seat beneath an arc-shaped lamp, which Mia imagined would feel like sitting on a moonbeam.

Fearfully, she stared across the vast room to the equally vast bed. Its smooth, unruffled surface made her think of it as an arena where, instead of ponies trotting around performing to music, countless women must have flaunted their magnificent bodies and demonstrated the sophisticated sexual tricks they'd picked up along the way. Wasn't he going to be awfully disappointed when he found out the truth about her? That she knew absolutely zero about sex.

But it was too late to back out now—and the truth was she didn't want to.

She jerked her hand round to the upper part of her back, wishing she'd attended more of those yoga classes which would have given her a bit of added flexibility as she struggled to locate the tip of the zip.

'Here, let me,' said Theo, his silken chest gleaming as he walked towards her.

'Honestly, I can manage on my own,' she squeaked, her face getting hotter as she tilted her head back to make it easier. Because she didn't want him touching her when she felt so disadvantaged and out of place. When the balance of sexual experience felt so heavily weighted in his favour. She needed to calm herself down. To steady her breathing and remind herself that this was what she really wanted—which it was—and everything would be fine.

Theo frowned as he undid the belt of his trousers and slid the zip down over his aching shaft, unable to shake off the feeling that this wasn't quite what he had been expecting. What *had* he been expecting? He had no idea—because he'd never thought it would happen and, in many ways, Mia was still an unknown quantity. He had let her closer than he'd ever let any other woman—before or since—yet he hadn't seen her for over half a decade. Which made her...unique. And, because he was a man who had experienced just about every permutation of seduction in the book, wasn't the novelty value of this encounter making his heart feel as if it wanted to explode?

He had thought she might flirt a bit more, or

play games. Tease him and provoke him with her sexual power—for she must be in no doubt about how much he wanted her. But she seemed almost *nervous* and, though he knew he could dissolve those nerves with one long kiss, she was making him curious enough to want to observe her behaviour rather than seek to change it.

At least she had managed to unzip her dress at last, her cheeks growing even more heated in the process. His breath caught in his throat as the flower-sprigged garment slid to the floor and he was confronted with the vision of Mia standing before him wearing nothing but her bra and pants. He ran his gaze over her generous curves with a mixture of awe and lust. How could he have forgotten how utterly magnificent she was? An abundance of creamy flesh was spilling over the top of a lace-edged bra which barely constrained her delicious breasts. A pair of surprisingly sensible panties adorned the luscious hips—but it was amazing how a garment which had clearly been chosen to support rather than enhance should manage to achieve both so effortlessly. He liked the faint curve of her belly and the soft lines of her arms.

'Don't look at me like that,' she beseeched and then seemed shocked at having spoken out loud.

'Like what?'

'Like...'

'Come on, Mia,' he reprimanded silkily as she

stemmed her words by biting down hard on her lip. 'Surely you and I go back far enough to enjoy the luxury of speaking the truth in the bedroom. What's wrong with the way I was looking at you?' He paused, and even though a shaft of jealousy sliced through his body like a hot blade, he forced himself to ask the question. 'Surely men must have looked that way at you before?'

Her expression of intense concentration was followed by one of wobbling uncertainty, and if Theo had been a gambling man he might have wagered a bet on her blurting out that this was a bad idea and then rushing from the room. His brow furrowed as he wondered if he would attempt to stop her, despite how much he was aching for her. He wasn't sure. Because wouldn't part of him have agreed that this was a very bad idea?

'I'm a virgin!' she burst out.

Theo froze.

'Please tell me I'm hearing things,' he said quietly.

'You're not. I'm a virgin. I've never... I've never had sex with anyone before. Obviously,' she said, with a shrugging attempt at humour which didn't quite come off.

Theo could feel the sudden pounding of his heart as his gaze bored into her, unable to shake off a surreal sense of disbelief. 'Why the hell didn't you tell me this before?'

'*When*, Theo? It's not the sort of subject you can casually introduce into the conversation, is it? Should I have announced it when I arrived? Or on the way to see my grandfather? Perhaps I could have slipped it in when we were enjoying a glass of lemon cordial, though obviously I would have needed to have waited until Sofia had left the room since I'm not sure how good her English is.'

Theo felt the boil of rage and frustration and the equally annoying sensation of being wrong-footed—and in the bedroom of all places. Why the hell hadn't he guessed, when the clues had been there for him to see all along? Didn't that explain the subliminal aura of innocence which always seemed to surround her—even after all this time? Or the sense of wonder she'd displayed when he'd kissed her earlier today, as if no man had ever kissed her like that before? He frowned. Had that really only happened a few hours ago?

'You should have told me,' he said flatly as he bent down to pick up his discarded shirt. 'Call me selfish, but I would have preferred not to have started all this, then been forced to stop.'

'Stop?' She was blinking at him. 'Who's talking about stopping?'

'I am!' He hauled the shirt on over his shoulders, needing to get out of that room as quickly as possible, unwilling to watch her put her dress back on and struggle with the damned zip and wriggle that delicious body until he was in danger of losing his mind. His throat constricted. 'Obviously, this changes everything,' he said tightly.

'Why?' she demanded. 'I mean, why does it have to?'

'I'm not having sex with a virgin,' he snapped.

She was shaking her head, the glossy spill of copper curls tumbling down over her shoulders, and he wondered if she had any idea how lovely she looked right then. No, he thought. One thing Mia could never be accused of was vanity. Hadn't her narcissistic mother cruelly punctured her self-confidence once too often, leaving her with none? Wasn't it time that he told her just how beautiful she really was?

'I still don't understand,' she whispered. 'You want sex with me and I definitely want sex with you. A piece of paper says we're legally married—so what's the problem? Please explain it to me.'

He chose his words carefully. 'The fact that you haven't been intimate with anyone else is significant.'

'How?'

He shrugged. 'It suggests you still care for me and will read too much into it,' he continued repressively. 'And I really don't want that to happen.'

Mia stared back, her heart slamming hard against her ribcage as she took in what he'd just said. 'Of all the arrogant things you've ever said to me, Theo Aeton—and there have been plenty of those,' she breathed, 'that one really tops the lot.'

'Is it arrogant to articulate my reservations?' he demanded. 'I thought we were being honest with each other.'

He used words very cleverly, Mia thought with reluctant admiration. Was her innocence too heavy a burden for a man like him to take on and was he going to rethink this whole marriage-with-sex idea?

And if he did, what then? Would they be expected to flit around the place pretending to everyone they were man and wife, and all the while existing in the same kind of state of frustrated celibacy they'd endured before? Was she going to allow that to happen for a second time?

No, she was not.

It dawned on her that she was standing there in nothing but a pair of pants and a bra, and that although Theo was clipping out logical reasons about why they *shouldn't* be having sex his eyes kept straying reluctantly to her cleavage. And didn't that make her feel good about herself for the first time in years? Or should that be bad? She wasn't sure.

She licked her lips and saw him watching *that* too, like a dog sitting patiently underneath the dining table, knowing that, a few feet away, a juicy piece of meat was being consumed. In the garden she had thought about her sexual power—which had now joined the list of stuff which was important to her, like self-worth and making her own way in the world.

And she realised that if she allowed Theo to dictate what happened next she would find herself back at square one. She would change back into someone docile and accepting—a person who allowed herself to be moved around like an object, rather than reaching out and taking what she really wanted. Which was him. It had always been him.

Her heart was beating very fast as she began to walk across the room and any shyness she might have felt at being half-naked was quickly melted by the hungry burn of his eyes. He said nothing as she approached and still nothing as she hooked her arms around his neck, brushing her lips against his.

'I won't read anything into it,' she said. 'This won't mean anything. I promise.'

He seemed to hold himself rigid and tense and for a moment she wondered if he was going to push her away, but then he gave a growl of what sounded like desire, underpinned with something she didn't dare focus on, in case it was resignation—or regret.

Or could it be submission?

Because now there was no slow striptease, or lazy and provocative smile from the man she had married. All that tight self-control had left his face. His expression dark with intent, he picked her up as lightly as if she were a sack of feathers rather than a stocky little maid, and carried her over to the bed.

He laid her down, his eyes not leaving her face as he tore off the unbuttoned shirt and it drifted to the floor out of sight. Her gaze followed the movement of his hand to the zip of his trousers, but she was determined not to betray any trace of shyness as he carefully eased it down.

And wasn't the truth that she *didn't* feel shy? Not a bit. They had indulged in plenty of foreplay in the shadowed and secret corners of her grandfather's estate, but they'd never got this far before. They'd never even entered any of the bedrooms—control freak Theo would never have allowed it.

But here they were. *Here they were.* And after so many stop-starts, Mia was determined to enjoy every second of it. As he kicked off his trousers and slid his shorts down to expose the massive shaft of his erection, she couldn't help thinking how *right* it all felt. Was it crazy of her to be happy she'd never done this with anyone else— and happy she had saved this part of herself for him? Of course it was. She wasn't supposed to be reading anything into it. Certainly not sentimental stuff like that.

He was naked at last and, greedily, she ran her

gaze over his incredible body. Honed muscle rippled beneath the olive-gold silk of his skin. The broad bank of his shoulders tapered down to a hard chest and narrow hips. His legs were long and athletic, his thighs powerful and strong. He was beautiful, she thought yearningly. There was no other way to describe him. And she had waited a long, long time for this moment.

The mattress dipped as he joined her on the bed and as she felt the hard brush of his leg against hers she felt the first faint shimmering of apprehension. She was scared of disappointing him. Scared of disappointing herself. Did he realise that? Was that why his black eyes became smoky and hooded as he bent his head towards her?

His kiss was everything she needed. Bcneath his seeking lips Mia eagerly opened up as his mouth drugged her into an instant state of compliance. She ran her fingertips over his arms, his shoulders, and the tight silken curve of his buttocks—as if she needed to touch him all over to make sure he was for real.

And he was.

So *very* real.

His hands were moving over her too and he clicked out a sound of rueful impatience as he encountered the lingerie she was still wearing. His fingers found the catch of her bra, which he released easily, so that her breasts came tumbling out into his hands and Mia gasped as he cupped them. His fingers were tracing circles over her nipples and every nerve-ending was firing into exquisite life. She squirmed with excitement beneath his questing touch and he drew his mouth away from hers.

'Always so responsive,' he murmured, looking down into her face. 'Every. Single. Time.'

Mia opened her mouth to say something—though she wasn't quite sure what her answer might be—but by then he had started sliding her pants down over her thighs and words became impossible. And suddenly she didn't care that she'd always thought her legs a bit like a rugby player's—because Theo was murmuring appreciatively as he kneaded his fingers over her skin, telling her she was beautiful. And right then, she *felt* beautiful as his fingers found her aching bud and began to stroke her with a delicacy of touch which was driving her crazy with equal amounts of pleasure and frustration. Could he tell how much she wanted him? Was that why he gave a low laugh as he delved deep into her honeyed heat, using the lubrication to slide slickly over her quivering flesh again, until she was writhing with unashamed need.

'Theo,' she breathed, because almost immediately she found herself on the brink of an orgasm, as she had been so many times before. 'Oh, God, Theo.'

But he withdrew his hand and pulled away, the faint shake of his head sending arrows of disappointment shooting up her spine.

'No. Not like this,' he informed her sternly. 'This time we do it properly.'

Or improperly, thought Mia dreamily, vaguely aware of him reaching for what was obviously a condom as she heard the tearing of foil. Did he always have one to hand? she wondered jealously. Through half-closed eyes she watched as he slid the protection on and she had to suppress the stupid thought that if they'd stayed married they might have had a little baby by now. Or a small child, even.

But then he was kissing her again and all those pointless thoughts dissolved. Everything was forgotten as her world became centred in this bed and what Theo was doing to her. His big hands had begun to explore her body, as if he were re-acquainting himself with every centimetre of her flesh. His rapt thoroughness thrilled her, even if he seemed curiously detached at times. A rush of liquid warmth flooded through her and he gave another murmur of appreciation as his fingers re-located its source. He licked her breasts, her belly and her thighs, though his mouth stayed poised above her aching bud and she could have screamed out loud with frustration.

Was his effortless self-control threatening to desert him? she wondered. Was that why he gave that almost angry little growl as he moved over her, the warmth and weight of his body making her feel deliciously fragile, for the first time in her life?

'Do you know how long I've waited for this?' he ground out harshly.

And now Mia could see that his self-control wasn't effortless at all. Judging by the tension which made his face look like dark marble, he only just seemed to be holding onto it by a thread. His eyes didn't leave her face as he positioned himself over her, but as she felt the broad tip of his hardness nudging against her molten heat, Mia quickly shut her eyes. Because what if all her love and longing came back the moment he entered her?

And then he did. Filling her with that first long, slow thrust. The pain was swift—forgotten almost as quickly as it had happened. Had she cried out? Was that why he stopped, his words an urgent imperative?

'Open your eyes, Mia.'

Tentatively, she obeyed, her lashes fluttering open to meet the gleaming black searchlight of his.

'Does it hurt?'

She shook her head. 'It did. A bit. But not now. Not any more.'

He swallowed. 'Does this?'

Soft heat began to filter through her veins as he began to move with infinite precision inside her. 'Oh, no,' she whispered, with breathless delight. 'That definitely doesn't hurt.'

His fingers tangled in her hair as kissed her and began to take up a rhythm, slowly at first, until her body had relaxed enough to accommodate him. On a purely anatomical level, it was astonishing that he was able to fit so comfortably inside her. And then she was done with analysing. Done with everything apart from what was happening to her. She was doing things she hadn't realised she knew how to do. Lifting her legs, she hooked her thighs around his back and he gave a low laugh of pleasure as he cupped her buttocks with the palms of his hands, and increased his speed. She gasped as he drove deeper inside her and he bent his head so that his warm breath fanned her lips.

'You like it like this?'

'Isn't it obvious?' she gasped. 'Do you like it too, Theo?'

'Isn't it obvious?' he ground out mockingly.

But when it happened it shocked her—because surely one orgasm was the same as any other, and Theo had made her come plenty of times in the past. But as her body contracted around his and he made a sudden choking moan which sounded almost…helpless… Mia realised she had been wrong.

Because this was different. *This* was intimacy. This man. Inside her. Her heart beating against his. Their flesh joined. Literally. The slowing pump of his seed. Just the thought of it blew her away. Made her grow soft with yearning.

But that way of thinking was spiked with danger and right now she didn't want anything spiky in her life—not when she could feel a delicious languor creeping over her. She felt sleepy and thoroughly satisfied. So she laid her head against Theo's chest and listened to the muffled thunder of his heart, and in that moment Mia felt something very close to contentment.

Theo lay with his eyes wide open as Mia slept against him, her head resting on his heart. He could feel the steady rhythm of her warm breath and feel the tickle of her hair, which curled like fiery snakes against the darkness of his chest.

He was tempted to stroke her magnificent breasts again but, despite the proximity of a peaking nipple, he resisted the temptation, grateful for this brief respite. Relieved to have been left alone with his thoughts, even though they were making him uncomfortable. He stared up at the ceiling, at the motionless blade of the fan which reminded him of the helicopter which had brought her here today. He thought how remarkable it was that, in a few short hours, the world as he knew it had changed.

His body was sated. He could never remember feeling so empty yet so satisfied, all at once. As if he had just devoured a delicious meal yet already his appetite was sharp and hungry for more. His body had begun to stir, the warmth of the naked woman in his arms making him grow harder with every second that passed.

His mouth was dry and he swallowed, but that did nothing to alleviate the dustiness of his throat. He could have reached out to pick up a glass of water from the bedside table but he didn't want to move. He needed to get his head straight before she woke and to put everything in perspective.

He sighed. He'd spent a long time wondering what sex with Mia would feel like and although everyone knew comparisons were odious, it was human nature to make them. And now he had made the unwelcome discovery that nobody compared to her. Because the sex had been...

Ever the perfectionist, he searched around for the right word. Sublime. *Neh.* He suppressed a bitter laugh. The best sex of his life. *And he didn't want it to be.* Hadn't he been hoping it would have been something of an anti-climax, especially when he'd discovered that she had remained a virgin? Hadn't he wanted it to be clumsy and forgettable?

But there had been no awkwardness or embarrassment, despite her inexperience. He could never remember kissing a woman as deeply as he had kissed Mia. Could never remember coming so hard, or for so long, of feeling as if she'd ripped out a fundamental part of him and exposed it to the light. His mouth hardened, as the desire to touch her again overwhelmed him and this time he did not resist. He ran his fingertips over her spine and as she murmured something incomprehensible against his chest, he started to play with her nipple, which obligingly sprang into life.

It was no big deal.

Of *course* it was going to feel amazing. Everyone knew there was nothing as effective as delayed gratification. Didn't he enjoy his own hard-earned wealth more than those of his contemporaries who had inherited theirs, because he'd known real hunger and real poverty? And so it was with Mia. He'd waited a long time for this. Again, he frowned. Of course he hadn't actually *waited*—for that would imply something had been missing from his life. Or that he'd intended for this to happen—which, of course, he hadn't. It had happened by chance—it wasn't some far-fetched concept of destiny, because there was no such thing. Just as there was no such thing as love, or happy families, or a whole list of meaningless things which people wasted precious time trying to attain. What the hell was a *soulmate* anyway? he thought contemptuously.

A sense of resolution crept over him. All he needed to do was to have as much sex with her as possible, before she flew back to her very different life in England. His lips hardened. A glut of intimacy would make their entrance into society as newly-weds that bit more convincing and it would also give this *thing* a chance to burn itself out.

And he wanted it to burn out.

He needed it to burn out.

He wanted her out of his head, once and for all.

Slipping his other hand between her thighs, he edged his thumb upwards to slide over her swollen bud and she wriggled her hips appreciatively.

'Theo,' she whispered, her breath growing more rapid as, delicately, he began to strum lightly against her satin heat.

'What?' he whispered as the smell of her sex filtered into the air and he breathed it in, like oxygen.

'I don't know,' she said drowsily. 'Just Theo.'

'Do you want me?'

Still she didn't open her eyes, but she opened her thighs. 'What do you think?'

But Theo didn't want to think. Not any more. He didn't want to do anything except be inside her. Deep and hard. Hot steel against cool silk. He wanted to make her scream, over and over. He wanted to imprint himself on her body so indelibly that any man who came after him would be incapable of giving her this much pleasure. But as he sheathed himself with another condom, he found himself consumed by a sensation he didn't recognise. A sensation which was powerful and all-consuming, which demanded definition.

It was delayed gratification, he reminded himself as he eased himself into her tight wetness.

Nothing more complicated than that.

CHAPTER EIGHT

MIA OPENED HER EYES. Outside the enormous and unfamiliar window the sky was as bright as a field of cornflowers, and in the distance she could see the sapphire sea glinting in the morning sunshine. Still drowsy, she looked around. She was lying on a huge bed, completely naked and completely alone. Spotting the ruffled sheet, which must have fallen to the ground, she reached down and hauled it up over her aching breasts, using her free hand to push back the tangle of curls which was flopping wildly over her face.

Like an animal in the undergrowth, she grew very still, listening intently for sounds— the whoosh of a shower, perhaps, or the brushing of teeth. But there was no sight or sound of the man who had spent the night giving her the kind of pleasure she'd only ever dreamed about. She plumped up the soft pillows and leaned back against them. They'd had sex so many times, she'd lost actual count. At one point—it must have been past midnight because none of the servants were in the house—Theo had gone down to the kitchen to forage for food because the grumbling of her stomach had made her realise she hadn't eaten a thing all day.

She had fallen on the Greek salad and delicious bread, the garlicky hummus and succulent slices of melon, and washed them down with some more of the lemon drink they'd had earlier. She remembered Theo watching her with a look of wry amusement on his face, telling her that it was rare to see a woman enjoying her food so much. She wasn't sure if she liked the sound of *that*. And when they'd had their fill, he had lifted a spoon to trickle some thick dark honey into her belly button and then spent a frustrating age licking it out, so that by the time his sticky tongue had flickered between her thighs, Mia had orgasmed almost immediately.

Anxiously, she glanced down at the sheet, looking for any tell-tale signs of their sexual antics—as a maid she was used to rapidly assessing the state of bedlinen—but thankfully there was no leftover honey to make the servants gossip.

She blanched. The servants! What would they say when they discovered—as they invariably would if they were doing their jobs properly— that her bed hadn't been slept in? Should she creep in there now and ruffle it up, the way they did in films?

Slumping back against the soft pillows, Mia expelled a huge sigh. None of this was supposed to have happened, and part of her despaired at how easily Theo had managed to manipulate her. For a start he had extracted her agreement that they would masquerade as a married couple, in order to please a dying man. How insane was that? And then he had seduced her. No. That would imply that what had happened had been one-sided, or that he'd had to persuade her, when the truth was that she had grabbed at the experience eagerly.

Had she really taken off her clothes in front of him, stubbornly refusing his help with her zip? Yes, she had. Had she really—this had been much later in the night, of course—taken him in her mouth and heard him moan with pleasure as she had swallowed the salty essence of him? Yes, that too. Again, Mia sighed. He had left her physically satisfied, but he'd left her feeling emotionally vulnerable too. Why else was she lying alone in this great big bed, feeling as if he had ripped away a layer of her skin, leaving her longing for the sort of things which were never going to happen? Come to think of it—where *was* he?

As if on cue, the door opened and Theo walked in, dressed in dark trousers and another pale silk shirt. His black hair looked damp and his skin gleamed like burnished gold. He looked full of energy and vigour, but his ebony eyes were cool and unfathomable.

'Good morning.'

His voice was cool, too, as if nothing out of the usual had occurred last night, and Mia's mushrooming vulnerability only increased, which probably explained why she didn't return his civilised greeting and came out with a blunt and needy question instead. 'Where have you been?'

He raised his eyebrows. 'I went for a swim.'

'A *swim*?' she questioned.

'*Fisika,*' he agreed equably. 'I always swim in the mornings. I think I already told you that? Then I came up here to shower and dress and you were still asleep and you looked...' A pulse briefly flickered at his temple. 'You looked so peaceful that I decided to go downstairs and do some work.' His smile was brief. 'I always find I'm more productive when the world is quiet.'

And he'd seen no reason to break his wretched routine? Mia wondered. No, of course he hadn't. Because this was nothing new to him. Certainly nothing like the earth-shattering experience it had been for her. She was just another woman in his bed—who knew nothing about post-sex morning etiquette. Which was why he had absented himself. He had probably been sending out a very deliberate message and helpfully reminding her that this wasn't a *real* relationship. So stop behaving like a wimp and show him your strength.

'I'm just wondering what happens now,' she said.

'In terms of…?'

Holding the sheet firmly against her aching breasts, she stared at him and all her determination to stay strong began to falter.

In terms of are you even going to bother kissing me, or does that only happen as a precursor to sex?

'I'm naked in your bed, Theo.' Mia paused, enjoying the sudden flash of fire in his eyes, which was the only chink in the cool mask he'd worn since entering the bedroom. Pushing her curls away from her face, she saw the flash in his eyes intensify. 'So naturally I'm wondering if anyone is around to see me going back to my own room, which is some distance away. Sofia, or Dimitra, for example.'

'And if they do see?'

'You must admit, it would be slightly awkward.'

'I agree, it might have been.' He paused, his jaw firming. 'Had I not gathered all the servants together after my swim and informed them of your true identity.'

Did he mean to make it sound as if she'd been taking part in a police line-up? Mia blinked. 'You've told them I'm your wife?'

'I did. We aren't intending to keep it secret, are we? My new maid actually giggled and, when I asked her why, told me she'd already guessed—apparently, she's friendly with someone who used to work for your grandfather back in the day.'

'Oh.' Mia stared at him blankly and the strangest thought stole into her head. That here she wasn't alone and anonymous. Here people actually knew her—or knew of her. That feeling of being rootless and disconnected briefly evaporated and she felt a brief burst of connection.

'So why don't you borrow my robe and get ready?' he continued, his velvety voice disrupting her introspection. 'After breakfast we'll go and see your grandfather to reinforce our *togetherness*. Strike while the iron is hot, as my English teacher used to say.' His eyes glittered. 'How does that sound?'

It sounded like a timetable. It sounded like Theo taking control just the way he always used to, but in this instance she was happy to let him. She needed to get her head straight and to work out the best strategy, going forward. Because obviously they were both coming at this marriage of convenience from different places. She had hoped for a kiss, or an echo of the enchantment they'd shared during the night.

But he had been...

She sighed.

He wasn't being unkind, no, but certainly no-body could mistake his matter-of-fact attitude for romance. And the only reason that might upset her was if she cared about him, and she didn't. She mustn't. That was the only thing she needed to remember. Because if she allowed herself to care for him, she was going to get hurt all over again.

'Great idea!' she said brightly, climbing out of bed to make her way across the room, glad her back was to him so he couldn't see her look of discomfiture, because she was acutely aware of her wobbly bottom.

Alone in the bathroom she was shocked by the face which stared back at her from the mirror. Those wide, dark eyes and kiss-bruised lips which indicated just how thoroughly she had been ravished—not to mention the wild disarray of her hair. She took a moment to untangle her curls and brush her teeth, finding a bathrobe and knotting it tightly around her waist before returning to the bedroom, hoping Theo might have gone down-stairs and spared them another awkward encounter.

But he hadn't gone anywhere. He was standing exactly where she had left him—as motionless as the glass statue on the other side of the room. The only thing which moved were his eyes and they flickered as they glanced at the robe which cov-ered her—way too big and flapping around her ankles—as if drawing attention to how much taller and bigger he was.

'Mia,' he said, his voice suddenly growing rough.

'I'm off to my room to have a shower,' she informed him as she passed him by, but he stalled her by catching hold of her wrist and encircling it within his own big hand. It was loose enough for her to break free, so why didn't she? Why was she revelling in the warm brush of his skin against hers, which was making her heart race as if she'd been sprinting for the bus?

'I don't think you want to go anywhere,' he contradicted silkily.

'Theo!' But the word was more of an incitement than a protest. She really had to stop saying his name like that because it was giving him the wrong idea. Or should that be the right idea? She swallowed, her eyes fluttering to an infuriatingly close as he bent his lips to her neck.

'Theo, what?' he murmured, the feel of his mouth against her skin inciting her even more.

'I th-thought…' she stumbled, before her sentence faded away.

'Mmm?' His tone was careless as he untied the oversized bathrobe and Mia's knees threatened to buckle as he began to play with her breasts. 'What did you think, my beauty?'

But it was impossible for her to remember. Her

brain had turned to mush and so had her body, especially as he was manoeuvring her over towards the bed and, oh, she wanted that. She wanted that *so much*. His lips had now moved to her mouth, that first taste causing him to pause.

'Did you use my toothbrush?' he questioned huskily.

Mia's eyelids snapped open and the sight of the raw desire on his face at last gave her the courage of her own convictions. 'Why shouldn't I?' she declared, ribaldly repeating what she'd heard some of the bolder chambermaids say at work. 'We've shared more than a bit of saliva during the night, surely.'

His corresponding laugh was low as he unzipped his trousers and let them fall, before sitting on the end of the bed and pulling her towards him. Mia moaned. She was wet for him. So hungry that she could barely wait until he had stroked on a condom. And then she was straddling him, gasping as he pulled her down onto the velvet-steel of his erection. And he was groaning as she tilted her hips and shifted her weight towards him, feeling him going deeper and deeper, until they were both choking out their pleasure at exactly the same time, and he muffled the sound of their cries with the hard press of his lips.

Her head lay heavy on his shoulder and reluctantly Theo loosened his hands from around her waist, though he could have stayed like that all morning, with the soft fan of her breath against his skin.

'I suppose I'd better go and get dressed,' she said drowsily, lifting her tousled head to survey him with sleepy eyes. 'See you at breakfast.' She yawned. 'Didn't Sofia say something about it being served out on the terrace?'

'That's right.' And even though his instinct was to peel her grapes and slowly pass them from his mouth into her own, he quashed it. 'You'll find everything you need.'

'But you'll be there?'

'No. I had some breakfast after my swim,' he added, feeling her soft body grow tense against his.

'Oh.'

'Come and find me afterwards,' he said, hardening his heart to the note of disappointment in her voice. 'I'll be working in my office. One of the staff will show you the way if you can't remember how to get there.'

'I'm sure I can manage to find my way around a private house—no matter how grand,' she retorted. 'After working in a two-hundred-and-fifty-room hotel.'

Despite her bravado, Theo couldn't miss the brief shadow of hurt on her lips, but although he told himself he didn't care, that wasn't strictly true.

She was starting to *get* to him and he didn't want that. He felt like a piece of soft clay in her hands, which she had begun moulding without first asking his permission. That was the reason why he had distanced himself from her this morning, after the intensity of the night they had shared. Those deliciously erotic hours in the moonlight, when it had been all too easy to forget how badly she had hurt him.

Ignoring the siren call of her body, he had left before she was awake, taking himself off to the pool to conduct a more punishing than usual early morning swim. After getting showered and dressed, he had walked in here intending to resist her, but resistance had been futile. One look at her and he had been lost. Despite his best intentions, he had lowered her onto his aching shaft, physical pleasure obliterating any concerns about his uncharacteristic lack of resolve.

Still, he thought, as he took his second shower of the morning—why not just go with the flow? He had spent far too much time already resisting Mia. Why not take as much as she was willing to give and reciprocate? Because, when the chips were down, was she really any different from any other woman? How could she be? With repeated exposure, her undeniable allure was bound to evaporate. He would become bored by her—it was as inevitable as the passage from night into day. His jaw firmed. And the sooner that happened, the better.

But when she appeared at the door of his home office an hour later, growing bored of her seemed too big a stretch of the imagination. Beneath his breath, Theo cursed, his immediate stirring of lust reinforcing how completely she had captivated him. How had she managed to maintain that air of shining sweetness, despite the decadent night they'd just enjoyed? Her copper curls were tamed into glossy ringlets, her cheeks flushed with roses and she was wearing another of those simple cotton dresses—this one awash with tiny bluebirds rather than flowers. She looked fresh and wholesome and, despite her undeniable effect on his senses, thoroughly out of place in the pared-down luxury of this house.

'I phoned Pappous's house,' she announced. 'And apparently he had the best night's sleep he's had in a long time.' Her voice grew soft. 'The nurse said how much better he looked this morning.'

Theo put his pen down. 'I'm pleased. And yesterday, he saw you.' He raised his brows. 'The two facts can't be unrelated.'

'I wouldn't dream of making that connection,' she responded quietly. 'But like you, I'm pleased.'

Shutting down his computer, he leaned back in his chair to study her. 'You know, before we go and see him, we need to arrange a shopping expedition.'

Her eyes narrowed with suspicion. 'What sort of shopping did you have in mind?'

'Things to wear, mainly.'

'For me?'

'Of course.' His gaze flickered to the same cheap espadrilles she'd been wearing yesterday and even though the ribbons tied around her slim ankles were undeniably cute, they were also undeniably frayed. 'And shoes, of course.'

'What's wrong with the ones I'm wearing?'

'There's nothing wrong with them, Mia.' There was a pause. 'But you're supposed to be my wife.'

'And you don't think I look the part?'

He raised his brows. 'Do you?'

She tilted her chin in a defiant gesture and once again, Theo felt his throat dry.

'You're saying you want me in silks and satins because my very ordinary cotton dress lets you down, is that it?' she demanded.

He shook his head. 'I think you look lovely as you are,' he said suddenly, and the brief delight which replaced her mulishness inexplicably stabbed at his heart. 'But you're dressed like a maid rather than as the wife of a billionaire, and not only will it make our supposed marriage unconvincing, you'll also run the risk of feeling out of place when I take you out.'

'And we can't have that, can we?' she said waspishly. 'Very well, Theo. Do your worst. Fix me up with some personal shopper or whatever it is you rich people do—though I warn you I don't have the kind of figure for clingy silk dresses, so I'll probably look even more out of place.'

'I'm not proposing dressing you up like a doll,' he said coolly. 'Just buying you something new, which looks like it hasn't happened in quite a while.'

'I've been saving up for my veterinary course, which I'm funding myself,' she said. 'And I don't need more than an abbreviated wardrobe.'

'Clothes which are scanty?' he hazarded, with the quick beat of expectation.

'Don't be facetious, Theo. I just don't want to buy a lot of *stuff*,' she elaborated. 'The bare minimum, in fact. I won't be…' Her rosy face crumpled, as if suddenly remembering the grim purpose behind her visit. 'Because Pappous is very sick, so I'm probably not going to be here for long, am I?'

'No,' he said, his voice heavy. He broke off, as his maid appeared in the doorway. 'Yes, Dimitra, what is it?'

'Would you like some more coffee, Kyria Aeton?' she questioned shyly, in her cautious English.

'No more coffee for me, thank you, Dimitra,' Mia said, with a soft smile. 'My breakfast was delicious and the flowers you put on the table are very pretty. Thank you so much.'

'*Parakalo,*' said Dimitra shyly, and her beaming smile as she scuttled from the room was something Theo had never witnessed before. Suddenly he imagined a very different kind of life, with a full-time woman in it who made the servants smile.

What was the matter with him? His career was on yet another upward trajectory. As one of the wealthiest men in Greece, he was highly respected by his peers, by politicians—even by various minor royal families to whom he had given financial advice over the years. His diary was full to bursting with invitations to the kinds of parties which, as a boy, would have seemed like an impossible dream to him. Next week he had been asked to give the keynote speech at a world-leading conference in Nice. His formidable reputation went before him and there was little in the world of venture capitalism he did not excel at.

His body grew tense.

Yet suddenly, all he could think about was Mia.

CHAPTER NINE

THE SHOP THEO took her to didn't look much like a shop and when Mia said as much, he laughed. With its gleaming frontage and sophisticated window displays, she thought the grand neo-classical building seemed more like a temple. Housed in the very centre of Athens, it wasn't far from Syntagma Square and the imposing parliament building which dominated it.

But despite her pleasure at being back in the hustle and bustle of the historic city, Mia found herself shivering as she stepped inside the air-conditioned interior of the department store, recognising it as the natural habitat of the very wealthy. How her mother would have loved it! It was filled with the same kind of women who had their nails regularly painted in the Granchester spa, with their tiny waists and skinny bodies which owed their sinewy muscularity to obsessive gym sessions and sustained denial of food.

Was she imagining every female customer and assistant turning to gaze at the man who towered by her side? No, she was not. Of course they were looking at him. It was as much as she could do not to stare at him herself, he looked so utterly delectable in the handmade charcoal suit, which drew attention to the muscular power of the body beneath. He had chosen not to drive today and the chauffeur-driven car which had brought them here only served to reinforce just how powerful and wealthy he was.

She was introduced to a terrifyingly sleek personal shopper and they were taken into a beautiful wood-lined room, lit by vast chandeliers and decorated with vases of blood-red peonies, which the shopper informed them came from Mount Parnassus.

'I'm terrified they won't have anything in my size,' Mia hissed to Theo, as all her old body insecurities came flooding back.

'We have plenty,' said the shopper, with a reassuring smile. 'Just wait and see.'

'You speak perfect English,' said Mia, going a little red.

'I would have great difficulty doing my job if I didn't,' said the woman gently.

As a runner was dispatched to bring back armfuls of clothes, Mia thought what a waste it was that she'd never studied the Greek language properly, in order to make herself understood in a land she had always loved. And yes, her mother had discouraged her—but she could have ignored her advice, couldn't she? Jasmine Minotis might have been a bad mother on many levels, but she was hardly going to punish her only child for *learning*, was she?

In front of an enormous mirror which ran the risk of cruelly highlighting every bump and blemish, Mia slithered into a day dress of filmy silk chiffon. Part of the problem had been with *her*, she realised. Everyone in her life—her grandfather, her mother and then Theo himself—had treated her as if she were a mindless object who could be moved around at will.

But she had allowed them to do that, hadn't she?

Even now, wasn't she allowing Theo to splash the cash and treat her as his puppet?

She sighed. No. She was discovering that there was always a different way of looking at things. Her grandfather was a crashing snob—he always had been—and she had seen the flicker of disapproval in his eyes yesterday, when he'd seen what she was wearing. Was it such a big ask to wear the sort of outfit which would make him happy?

When she looked into the mirror, she was slightly taken aback by what she could see. She had imagined the fancy fabrics the shopper had guided her towards would do little for her voluptuous shape, but it seemed she had been wrong. Cleverly, the woman had selected a more upmarket version of her existing wardrobe for her approval. The delicate material was exquisitely cut—especially on the bust and hips. It enhanced her body in a way which flattered and the dark green suede shoes she chose made her stand differently. Walk differently. Suddenly, she was filled with a new-found sense of confidence and self-belief.

'How's this?' she questioned, pulling back the red velvet curtain before swishing into the room, and when Theo looked up from his laptop, Mia felt a sudden tightening of her heart as she saw his unguarded expression. Had she imagined the brief spear of pensiveness which had replaced the habitual flintiness of his black eyes? Didn't he used to look at her that way in the past?

But just as quickly his gaze became shuttered, his slow speculative smile indicating that there was nothing other than sex on his mind.

Of course it was.

Exactly the same thing as was on hers, she told herself fiercely.

Soon a small collection of purchases began to pile up. More dresses. A couple of swirly skirts and gossamer-fine blouses. A denim jacket. Sandals and shoes. But no trousers.

'I don't want to see you in trousers,' Theo growled. 'It is a crime to cover up legs like yours.'

And even though Mia knew this was an outrageous thing for him to say, she couldn't deny the thrill it gave her—particularly when she saw the shopper's expression of dreamy appreciation. But didn't plenty of women fantasise about masterful men who expressed distinctly unfashionable sentiments? She swallowed. Guilty, as charged.

Keeping on her favourite of the dresses—and the green suede shoes—she returned to the outer sanctum, where Theo was tapping out a message on his phone.

'Could you have the car drop me off after you go to the office?' she asked him.

'Or I could delay going into the office.' He slid the phone in his pocket and glanced at his watch. 'And we could have some lunch. There's a very good restaurant on the sixth floor.'

'Is this all part of the PR campaign?' she suggested wryly as they took the elevator up to the top floor. 'Showing off your "wife" in all her new finery?'

'Or could it possibly be because I thought you might be hungry?'

She tilted her head to one side. 'You associate me with appetite, do you, Theo?'

'I do,' he concurred, dark eyes glinting. 'All the appetites.'

'Oh. Are you flirting with me, by any chance?'

'I am,' he answered throatily.

But even as Theo acknowledged her quick smile of pleasure, loud warning bells were beginning to sound in his head. Because nothing was turning out as he had anticipated. He had long forgotten any ideas about punishing her for her desertion, but in place of revenge had come a relationship which confounded him. They were angry with each other for a lot of the time, yet she had given her virginity to him and blown his mind in the process.

Were they enemies with benefits? Was that an accurate description?

He gave a ghost of a smile as they were shown to a prime table in the window of the restaurant, where he ordered for both of them, at Mia's behest. While they waited for their meals to arrive, two glasses of pink champagne were delivered to the table and Theo stared at the fizzing flutes in bemusement. 'I didn't order these.'

'No, sir,' said the beautiful young waitress. 'But Kyrios Pavlidis has just telephoned. He heard you were here and wanted to extend his congratulations to you and your wife.'

'Efharisto,' said Theo, and the waitress smiled back before turning to deal with another customer.

'Who is she talking about?' questioned Mia, running her finger along the twisted stem of the glass.

'Vangelis Pavlidis. He owns the store and many

more like it.' He gave a short laugh. 'Word certainly gets around quickly that I'm out on the town with my wife.'

'I thought that was the whole point,' she observed crisply. 'New clothes and a very public lunch will give credence to our fake marriage, which will ultimately make my grandfather happy. It's a win-win. Isn't that so, Theo?' But her voice grew softer as she clinked her glass against his and took a sip of champagne, miming startlement as some bubbles dissolved against her nose. 'What time are we planning to see him?'

There was a pause as a click of warning shuttered into Theo's mind. He thought about the woman who had reared him and used him as a meal ticket. When he hadn't been foraging on her behalf, he had been instructed to stay out of the way as much as possible while she entertained her increasingly rowdy and casual boyfriends. He never remembered her cuddling him, or being kind to him, and it took a long time for him to stop hoping she would instead of accepting the grim reality. But that had been his life and he needed to accept it—not behave like a cuckoo in the nest, trying to muscle in on Mia's life. '*We* aren't planning anything,' he said suddenly.

'But you said—'

'That we'd both go, *neh*. But I've changed my mind. I'll go later, on my own. It's better that way.'

He steeled himself against the confusion in her eyes. 'It's you he wants to see,' he said roughly. 'Not me.'

She put her glass down with a bump, so that more pink bubbles fizzed to the top of the glass. 'But he'll want to see you, too! You're like family, Theo. You know you are.'

'No,' he negated harshly. 'That's where you are wrong. I have a particular relationship with him, that's all. I'm more like an employee.'

'No—'

'*Yes,*' he interrupted firmly. 'He enjoys my success and I have served as his conduit into the world of business, particularly after he retired. But it hasn't all been plain sailing. As you know, he can be an extremely difficult man, with traits I am prepared to tolerate because I have grown fond of him over the years and because his generosity is a debt which can never properly be repaid.' Theo felt the sudden race of his heart. 'But he is not my family, Mia—and he never will be. I don't *do* family. Don't you understand what I'm saying to you? I don't know how to do family. And neither do I want to.'

Mia bit her lip for the vitriol of his words was hard to hear—not just because of the anger but because of the underlying pain which had distorted his voice. She wanted to reach across the table and lay her hand over his but his body language was so forbidding that she didn't dare. And wasn't it weird how tension could kill off your appetite?

Their salads arrived and she stared uninterestedly at the glistening red tomato, white feta and gleaming black olives, before raising her eyes to his.

'Are you hungry?' she said.

There was a pause before his dark gaze was briefly directed towards the plate. 'Not for this, no.'

His words were razor-edged silk and his black eyes were glinting with something raw and hot, which Mia recognised instantly. Desire. It was pulsating through the air between them like honey and making her achingly aware of her body beneath the filmy dress. Suddenly Mia started teasing him. Encouraging him. Wanting him. She wanted him so much. 'What are you hungry for, then?' she murmured.

He didn't answer. He was calling for the bill. And besides, Mia didn't need an answer. Not a verbal one, anyway. Everything she wanted to know she could read in his tense, hard features. They got into the car but he didn't talk to her, or hug her or kiss her. Instead he slid his fingertips beneath the filmy layers of her brand-new dress and played with her aching bud until she was closing her eyes and murmuring a plea which sounded like his name, as he continued with his light and teasing rhythm. She gasped, her fingernails digging into the soft leather of the car seat, but just as she was about to come, he withdrew his hand, and her eyes snapped open to gaze in dazed disbelief as he shook his head.

'Not here,' he said softly.

'Wh-why not?'

'I would prefer to wait until we are in the bedroom.'

Mia stared at him in confusion. 'So is this about you losing control, or taking it?'

He looked at her consideringly. 'Does it really matter?'

Mia tensed, reminding herself that this was only supposed to be a temporary relationship so, no, it shouldn't matter. Yet somehow it did. It reminded her that Theo was calling all the shots, just as he'd always done.

She realised she was in danger. Of thinking and behaving like a *real* wife and she needed to stop all that right now. The most sensible and dignified reaction would be to tell him to go to hell when they got back to his estate and take herself off somewhere on her own. But her gnawing sexual hunger overrode every other consideration. To hell with dignity, she thought distractedly as the blood pounded hotly in her veins. To hell with everything. Her heart was racing as they mounted the stairs towards his suite, but neither of them said a word. The door sounded loud as he kicked it shut behind them, but once they were enclosed in the private world of his bedroom, Theo didn't move from the spot. His black gaze was flickering over her like dark fire, making her tremble wherever it lingered and burned.

'Take off your clothes,' he instructed softly.

This was nothing to do with control and everything to do with power, she recognised. His, versus hers. Was that because he had allowed her to see a glimpse of unfamiliar vulnerability when he'd talked about family earlier? Was it that which had resulted in this heartless but very sexy battle of mental domination?

She wondered what he would say if she refused—if she told him she'd changed her mind— but deep down she suspected he would simply shrug. Maybe tell her he really didn't have time for lunchtime sex anyway, and he'd see her later. And Mia thought she would die if that happened. She was so hot—so *eager* for him to touch her— that she did exactly as he asked.

She thought how much things had changed since yesterday, when he had taken her virginity with one delicious thrust and she'd been stricken with nerves. Yet today she no longer felt like a novice in his presence and today, she didn't struggle with her zip. It slid down with fluid ease and her dress fell to the floor with a whisper. She heard his ragged breath, as if finding himself suddenly short of oxygen, and as she glanced up to see the frustration on his face she assumed an expression of mock innocence.

'Oh. Didn't you realise I was buying new lingerie as well?' she questioned, cupping her breasts with her palms, the movement pushing them forward to emphasise the deep plunge of her cleavage against soft apricot lace. 'The shopper insisted the new clothes would look much better with the correct foundations underneath and I think she was right, don't you? Although I don't know whether these panties actually qualify as *foundation*, do you?' She did a little twirl, anxious for him to see her matching thong. 'Theo? Theo! What do you think you're doing?'

'You know damned well what I'm doing,' he roared as he picked her up in his arms and carried her over to the bed, before laying her down in the centre of it with hands which were distinctly unsteady.

And things seemed to have changed for him too, Mia realised. Maybe it was because she *was* no longer his virginal wife. Did he consider her his sexual equal now? Was it that which was making him treat her with such…? Mia gasped. Was there such a thing as tender roughness? Oh, God. There must be. She sucked in a breath as he squeezed her breast. How else would you describe it? She fell back against the soft pillows and, when she saw him undoing his belt, instinctively closed her eyes to increase the sensory experience and block out the tumult of her thoughts.

She heard the rasp of his zip and the tearing of foil as he pushed his trousers down to his ankles. Somehow she knew this was going to be quick and urgent, and she was right. He didn't even bother to remove her panties, her exultant little shout encouraging him to shove aside the moist panel and plunge straight into her waiting heat.

She moaned with pleasure at the sheer *intensity* of it. 'Oh, Theo,' she breathed and then, more brokenly as he moved inside her, 'Th-Theo.'

His eyes were dark, almost...*wounded*, she thought distractedly as he stared into her eyes before bending his face to hers, and his kiss seemed unbearably sweet and unbearably sad, all at the same time. He pushed deeper and filled her. His hands were in her hair, he was groaning and so was she. She felt the building of expectation. Of layer upon layer of pleasure, taking her higher and higher—until it was too much to bear any longer, and as she felt herself contracting around his rocky and pulsating shaft she called out his name.

At last, their bodies spent, he pulled her against him and she nestled into his hard warmth, her finger sliding over his silk shirt as she breathed in his heady masculine scent. She thought he must be sleeping, when suddenly he spoke, his words muffled by the thickness of her curls.

'Do you want to come to Nice with me next week?'

Fractionally, she pulled away to meet the dark gleam of his eyes. 'Why would I want to do that?'

'Because you're my wife and that's the kind of thing wives do?'

'Isn't that taking method acting a bit too far?'

The trace of a smile played at the edges of his lips. 'How about me wanting to see you lying in a tiny bikini by the edge of an extravagant swimming pool?'

'I don't wear tiny bikinis,' she said repressively.

'You should, especially since you look so good in a tiny thong.' His finger slid over the curve of her hip. 'I'm speaking at a conference and it's a great city. Ever been there?'

His question punctured her bubble. Would his lip curve with scorn if she told him the only time she'd ever been to France had been on a day-trip to Calais, organised by boss of the Granchester, who paid for his employees to have a fun day out every Christmas?

But Mia wasn't trying to score points, or to contrast their very different lifestyles. She was masquerading as his wife to please her grandfather. The tricky part was discovering how much she liked being with the man she had married, despite his mercurial nature.

'Sure, why not?' she agreed coolly, as if her heart weren't thumping with dread at the thought of how much she was going to miss him and she wondered why, of all the men she could have fallen for, it had to be him.

It had only ever been him.

She swallowed. Sometimes powerful emotions and feelings came out of nowhere but you didn't have to let them take you prisoner, did you? Because she was strong. *Remember that*, she told herself fiercely. *You've changed.*

She tried to rationalise why going to Nice would be a sensible move.

'I guess it will make our reconciliation look all the more convincing if we can't bear to be apart,' she hazarded.

'I guess it will,' he agreed, lying back against the pillows, his arms cushioning his dark head.

Mia jumped out of bed and headed for the bathroom, aware of his gaze on her. But to her delight, she didn't feel a bit shy about her semi-clothed state or that very urgent bout of lovemaking. In fact, it was easy to exult in Theo's very obvious approval. Perhaps he was teaching her to love *herself*—even if he didn't love *her*. Wouldn't that be something positive she could take away from all this?

There was no sign of him when she emerged from the bathroom, her appearance suitably repaired, and she was driven to see her grandfather who, as the nurse had promised, was noticeably brighter than yesterday.

'You're out of bed, Pappous,' Mia said, trying to iron the emotional wobble from her voice. 'This… this is fantastic. *You* look fantastic.'

'*Neh*. I am like Lazarus,' the old man proclaimed, with a touch of his old arrogance. 'I have risen from the dead!' With a mischievous look, he complimented her on her new dress and asked if she wanted to drink some *soumada*. But Mia didn't want their precious time to be interrupted and so she shook her head and sat down beside him. For a moment there was silence, until at last they began to talk.

They discussed things which had always been taboo before and for Mia it was painful to listen to at times. He talked about her father. About the adorable little boy who had grown up to be so troubled. He talked of his guilt at never being able to help his son conquer his demons. He told her he was sorry to have cut her out of his life so ruthlessly, but that he'd been hurt, and bewildered because he thought she and Theo made a perfect couple.

'I still do,' he added gruffly. 'He is a good man, Mia.'

But she quickly changed the subject and, although she felt a little ashamed at the way they were deceiving him by pretending to be reconciled, didn't his evident contentment make it worth it? Instead she remarked on how well Tycheros was looking. And the dog, which lay close by her feet whenever possible, lifted his head on hearing his name, and licked at her hand.

The day before she left for Nice, Mia felt a sense of resolution. She kissed her grandfather goodbye and whispered that Theo would call in to see him after work and as she saw the old man's nod of approval, she was aware that she sounded like a real wife. She probably looked like one, too, with a stupid smile plastered all over her lips as she remembered that tonight she and Theo were planning to dine beneath the stars, and afterwards he would take her upstairs and they would reach for those very stars which blazed down with unpolluted white fire.

She reached down to tickle Tycheros's ears, when her warm feeling of satisfaction was punctured by another nagging splinter of doubt. For the first time since she'd arrived in Greece, Mia was beginning to get worried, because nothing was turning out as she'd thought it would.

Quite apart from the fact that she'd never been intending to have sex with Theo, this trip and this *marriage* were supposed to be time-limited—her brief tenure defined by her grandfather's precarious state of health. There had been a beginning and there was supposed to be an end—except the end was no longer in sight. A miracle seemed to have happened and the old man had recovered much of his former vigour. And while that brought Mia great joy, it also brought her pain. And fear.

She wanted Georgios to live for as long as possible—of course she did—but she couldn't remain here indefinitely, pretending to be Theo's wife and allowing her emotions to be compromised with every second that passed. Because he was invading her thoughts and occupying her mind. Her heart and her body were full of him.

She walked through the overgrown rose bower towards the waiting car, clenching her hands into tight little fists, as the reality of her situation was revealed to her—like a thick layer of dust being removed from a mirror.

Because suddenly Mia realised that she had walked into a trap of her own making. Proximity had a power all of its own and so did passion. And if she didn't start protecting herself, she could get badly hurt.

CHAPTER TEN

'WHAT WE NEED to ask ourselves is...' Theo paused, his delivery crisp and precise as he looked around the gilded room, at all the privileged faces who were watching him so raptly '...do we really want our children and our grandchildren accusing us of being the generation who knew the cost of everything, and the value of nothing?'

A split second of silence greeted his closing words, before the jammed room started applauding. People were on their feet. Beneath the stained glass of the domed ceiling, shouts of *'Bravo!'* and *'Encore!'* were echoing. A beautiful brunette he half recognised was blowing him a kiss. Theo's gaze scanned the room for Mia, alighting at last on her diminutive form standing at the back of the room, beneath the portrait of an early French king. He thought she looked a little...*anxious* and he frowned. What was making the little maid appear so uncomfortable?

He really needed to stop thinking about her that way, he told himself fiercely, focussing instead on her resilience, her independence and pride. And, of course, the enduringly soft and kittenish appeal which lay beneath her feisty new exterior. A softness which invoked in him a powerful protectiveness—a response he kept telling himself was inappropriate under the circumstances. Because Mia didn't need his protection. She had made her feelings very clear during their two-day stay at Nice's most magnificent hotel, which overlooked the famous Promenade des Anglais.

She had been...

What?

His brows knitted together, because it was difficult to put his finger on. She had charmed everyone she'd met and shown a very real appreciation of their five-star hotel—despite mentioning something about the alignment of cushions, which he gathered had not met with her approval. Their lovemaking had been as exquisite as always. So what was it?

He frowned.

Something he hadn't expected.

Ever since they had arrived, she had been behaving with a certain detachment towards him, which was usually *his* thing. She had been watchful and wary. She had seemed...distant. And while none of those things should matter to him, he was finding that they did. His eyes narrowed as he crossed the room, fielding the many pats on the back he received as he made his way towards her.

He noticed several women watching his progress, yet not one of them had a fraction of the appeal of the petite redhead in the floaty dress. Her fiery curls were piled haphazardly on top of her head, several tumbled strands giving her a delicious just-got-out-of-bed look. Which to some extent was accurate. Not in the least tempted by the many enticements this famous seaside town had to offer, they had spent the majority of their time in bed.

His throat constricted. He had tasted her, sucked her, drunk her and eaten her. She was like a non-stop feast he couldn't seem to stop devouring because he couldn't get enough of her. How had she managed to do it—this innocent and unpretentious young woman? To have woven such a spell of enchantment, that at times he couldn't think straight?

'Mia,' he said as he reached her. 'How do you think my speech went?'

'Well, obviously, your peers loved it.' A little self-consciously, she adjusted the strap of her sundress. 'I've never heard applause like that, outside of a concert. Mind you, I don't think I've ever listened to a forty-minute talk on venture capitalism before.'

He made an impatient clicking gesture with his fingers. 'And?'

Mia chose her words carefully. She'd been doing a lot of that since they'd got here—walking over verbal eggshells, so to speak. Since she'd been in Nice it had seemed vital that she distance herself from him as much as possible. Not in an obvious way. In bed, she was no different—her sexual response to him as ecstatic and enthusiastic as it had always been. But she was trying hard to focus on all the reasons why Theo was not a good long-term bet—the biggest one being that their marriage was nothing but a farce, a temporary union which would be dissolved as soon as her grandfather died.

Because it was funny how being in a different location made you look at things in a different way. She looked around, listening to the rising buzz as the sophisticated audience chattered among themselves in the dome-ceilinged room. She wasn't like these people. She'd observed their reactions when she had been introduced as Theo's wife. The quick double-take before looking her up and down as if they might have missed something, first time round. As if wondering why the man who could have anyone had settled for someone like her.

Why had he brought her here? He certainly hadn't needed to. As far as she could make out, there were hardly any other wives or partners at the convention.

But that wasn't a question to ask him now, in this public arena—not when he was regarding her thoughtfully, his jet-dark eyes narrowed, as if he had picked up on the unease which had been growing for days now. She thought about the concluding words of his speech and a terrible sense of inevitability began to ripple up inside her as she acknowledged why she had found them so disturbing. Because things were coming to a head, weren't they? That was what happened in life. Nothing ever stayed the same.

'You were brilliant,' she said. 'You know you were.'

He smiled. A tight, hard smile which pierced through her emotional armour without any obvious effort on his part.

They returned to their lavish suite, with its wall of windows overlooking Nice's glittering coast. When they had arrived it had felt a bit like a honeymoon destination, because it was quite obviously the finest accommodation in the upmarket establishment. But now, the magnificent view of the Promenade des Anglais left Mia cold, as did the golden glimmer of the walls and the amazing artwork, which must have been worth a fortune. She might as well have been in a railway waiting room for all the notice she took of her surroundings.

While Theo put in a call to his office, she went into the bathroom, her heart thumping as she gazed into the mirror, knowing she couldn't keep on blotting out questions which needed to be asked, just because she was afraid of what the answers might be.

So was she going to ask him? Or was she just going to keep burying her head in the sand?

She found him outside on the vast expanse of terrace, gazing out at the turquoise glitter of the sunlit sea. He had removed his jacket and was leaning on the wrought-iron railings, looking utterly magnificent against the iconic backdrop. The rich sunlight highlighted the ebony darkness of his hair and illuminated the powerful body she knew so well. She stood very still for a moment, committing the delicious image to memory, but he must have heard her for he turned. His shuttered expression was unreadable, his hard face shadowed.

'You look troubled,' he observed slowly.

'I suppose I am,' she answered, slightly surprised by his question because wasn't that a bit *probing* for Theo?

'And why's that?'

'Think about it.' She lifted up her hands in exasperation. 'Most people might say that *pretending* to be married is stressful enough, but there are plenty of other things which have the ability to keep me awake in the middle of the night.' She paused, the tip of her tongue travelling over her bottom lip. 'Which I don't suppose you'll want to discuss. I thought your speech was brilliant, by the way.'

His intelligent black eyes gleamed, as if he was perfectly aware that she was stalling. 'So you said.'

'You ended it by talking about children.' She swallowed. 'And grandchildren.'

His expression was still closed and shuttered. 'I did. What of it?'

'You created a very powerful image with your words.'

'That's the secret of giving a talk which doesn't make people want to fall asleep.' Above the obsidian glitter of his eyes, his dark brows rose. 'But I suspect my use of powerful imagery isn't what's troubling you.'

'No.' Just *say* it. 'Do you want children of your own, Theo? Was that what made you address it?'

He shook his head. 'No.'

'And have you ever…have you ever wanted them?'

There was silence. 'You mean, with you?'

Mia's heart was beating so loud she was surprised he couldn't hear it. Surely the whole hotel could hear it. She nodded.

'Yes, I wanted a family,' he said at last. Raking his fingers back through the liquorice thickness of his hair, he expelled a long and ragged breath. 'A real family, like I'd never known. A happy family. When I still believed such a thing could exist.' He gave a bitter laugh. 'I wanted everything with you, Mia. Or at least, I thought I did.'

'Everything?' she verified breathlessly, even though her heart was breaking to hear him refer to it in the past tense.

'Of course.' His mouth twisted into a bitter smile. 'Because I was young and idealistic and you exemplified everything I'd never known in a woman before. You entranced me. Fascinated me. I was bowled over by your innocence and compassion and the way you never judged me, when I had been judged for all of my life. And you adored me.' A smile tinged with regret played at the edges of his lips. 'You left me in no doubt about that. You didn't hold back from telling me you loved me because you were waiting for me to say it first. You didn't try to manipulate my emotions. You were everything I thought a woman should be.' He paused. 'A black and white drawing on a piece of canvas,' he finished quietly. 'Which I coloured in to fit my own specifications.'

'I'm afraid that kind of imagery is beyond me,' she breathed. 'I don't understand.'

'No. I didn't understand it myself for a long time.' Theo turned to look out at the sea, as if he might find the answer somewhere within the glittering dance of the waves, but he saw nothing other than swimmers splashing around in the shallows. And when he faced her again he could see that Mia's face had grown pale and her eyes were dark and huge, as if she already knew she wasn't going to like what he was about to say. But she had asked him, hadn't she? And since she had asked, she should listen to his answers. It might hurt her—and maybe it would hurt him, too—but it might enable them both to move on.

'I idealised you,' he said slowly. 'I made you into the woman I wanted you to be. That's why I insisted you came to our marriage as a virgin—not because your grandfather would be angry—'

'Well, he would.'

'*Neh, neh,* I know that,' he said impatiently. 'But my main motivator was that a virginal bride fitted my view of perfect womanhood. I looked on it as an old-fashioned arranged marriage. That's why I never told you I loved you, even though I knew how much you wanted me to,' he continued, and now his words became heavy. 'Because I didn't.'

'You…didn't?' she choked out, though the expression in her eyes suggested he was only confirming what she already knew.

'No. But don't take it personally. I'm not capable of loving anyone, Mia, and since you were nothing but a figment of my imagination how could I possibly love someone who didn't really exist?'

He could see her throat working.

'But you didn't really exist either, did you,

Theo?' she whispered. 'You married me because you claim to have wanted a happy family, but you weren't prepared to contribute anything to get it, were you?'

'I was earning—'

'I'm not talking about *money*! Everything with you comes back to the money, doesn't it?' she yelled. 'I'm talking about emotion! All the emotion you held back, like a miser hoarding his gold.' She sucked in a ragged breath. 'How can you possibly bring children into this world if you aren't prepared to show them love?'

'Maybe because I didn't know how?'

'But you're an intelligent man. You could have learnt.'

'You really believe that, do you?' he questioned mockingly. 'That love is something you can be taught—like maths, or tennis?'

'That's what I had to do. To teach myself,' she said simply. 'Because I never got any at home, either.'

And suddenly Theo was reminded of the first time he'd seen her. How, behind her tenderness towards the wounded puppy, he had detected a deep sense of hurt in her eyes. A sense of being alone, which he had identified with. He had wanted to reach out and tell her that, but something had stopped him. It was stopping him now and it always would. Because he couldn't give her what she needed. And she couldn't give him what he wanted. He didn't want her world of messy emotion, and pain.

'What's done is done,' he said, with brutal finality. 'And there's no point in raking over it.'

'I agree. Which is why we really can't continue with this farce of a marriage. I can't stay here like this—playing this fictitious role as your wife, which is going to get more complicated the longer it goes on. I need to go back to my real life. I feel...' She dragged in a breath. 'I feel so happy to have seen Pappous and I'm very grateful that you made me come here. The fact that my visit has coincided with, or caused him to enjoy, better health is, of course—wonderful. But now it's starting to scare me.'

Theo frowned. 'Why?'

'Can't you work it out for yourself? Because we've deceived him.' She bit her lip and he could see the shimmer of tears in her eyes. 'How is he going to react when he finds out what we've done? He'll probably be hurt and angry. Dear God—the shock could kill him.'

He shook his head. 'Your grandfather is made of stronger stuff than that,' he negated.

'You hope.'

Theo allowed his mind to assimilate all the facts, as if this were nothing but a question of logistics, and the sweet tremble of her lips undoubtedly influenced his next question. 'You wouldn't consider staying on—at least until your course starts in September? Like I said, I could easily have my office arrange for someone to cover your housekeeping role.'

'You mean…carry on?' She stared at him. 'Like this?'

'Is "this" really so bad, then, Mia?' he mocked softly. 'Good sex. Good company. I could live with that for a while longer. Couldn't you?'

She was shaking her head, the glossy curls glowing like a sunset. 'You just don't get it, do you, Theo?' she breathed.

Should he ask her to elaborate? Behind the set line of his lips, he gritted his teeth. No. He didn't want her to highlight their differences or present him with a catalogue of complaints about his behaviour. He just wanted this conversation to end, and for that they needed to decide what to tell Georgios when they got back to Greece. The truth, probably. No more lies. The important thing was that the old man had healed the rift with his granddaughter and nothing else really mattered. Mia would go and he might miss her, but it would only be for a while. He'd had sex with her now. She was no longer a mystery. And she knew now that he had never loved her.

Her phone began to ring and shattered the silence, but she ignored it.

Almost immediately, his own began to clamour. 'I'd better…' he said.

Her face was filled with scorn. 'Of course.'

But this wasn't the welcome interruption of work. He knew it was bad news the moment he accepted the call. A number and a voice he didn't recognise, filled with the careful compassion of someone doling out professional sympathy. He listened for a while in a state of unnatural calm and when he had terminated the call, he looked into Mia's sea-blue eyes, trying to find the right words.

'You'd better sit down,' he said heavily.

'I don't want to sit down. Tell me, Theo. Just tell me.'

And even though her pale cheeks made him suspect she had already guessed, he nodded. 'I'm afraid it's your grandfather,' he said, swallowing down the sudden lump which had constricted his throat. 'He died a few minutes ago.'

He wanted to take her in his arms and comfort her, but deep down he knew he didn't have the right, not after everything he'd said.

And touching her was always fraught with complications.

CHAPTER ELEVEN

THEO BARELY SAID a word to her, throughout the journey to Greece. Not on the plane, nor in the waiting car which took them straight to the funeral parlour. He had sat gazing out of the window, seemingly lost in thought. His face, Mia thought, looked as if it had been carved from some dark and unforgiving piece of granite. His features were bleak and stony, his body language forbidding. Was this his way of dealing with the grief of Georgios' passing? Had it made him close in on himself even more? Unable to offer her even the most rudimentary element of comfort?

She had not shared his bed. She had not shared so much as a kiss or a hug, since news had reached them in the south of France, right after their uncomfortable showdown which had left her in no doubt about how little she really meant to him. Perhaps with her grandfather gone, he no longer saw the need to maintain any kind of masquerade.

And didn't that make sense, on so many levels? The need for pretence was gone.

But she took her lead from him, clinging onto her composure and not giving into tears—not once. Not because she was afraid of showing her grief in front of the man who was still technically her husband, but because she was afraid that once she started crying, she might never stop.

Wearing the black dress and shoes which had been hastily purchased from the hotel boutique in Nice, Mia prepared to say her final farewell to her *pappous*.

'Do you want me to come in with you?' Theo asked.

Of course she did. She'd never even seen a dead person before. She wanted him to stand by her side and squeeze her hand. And afterwards hold her tight and dry her tears, and offer her the condolence she so badly needed.

But she didn't articulate her wishes because she was afraid of sending out the wrong message. To Theo, yes—but, more importantly, to herself. That might imply she was expecting him to behave like a real husband, or that she had started to rely on him, and was looking to him for support. And why get used to something which was only going to be snatched from you?

'No. You go in after me,' she said. 'I'll be fine.'

At least Theo took over all the funeral arrangements—booking the church, contacting friends, and putting notices in the paper—and Mia was grateful for his cool efficiency. The church was full, bright with the light of the candles which every mourner held. In a daze, Mia greeted them all—some she knew, though many she didn't. She recognised most of the nurses and thanked them for their care, and the first crack in her carefully constructed composure came when she was hugged by Georgios's old housekeeper, Elena. And that was when she had crumbled. Clinging to the matronly woman who had known her since she was young, she had sobbed her heart out.

The rest of the wake passed in a blur and Mia was dry-eyed by the time she slid into the passenger seat beside Theo and he drove her back to his house. But when she stood in a hallway in the light of the setting sun, she suddenly felt as if she'd lost her way—like someone stumbling around a maze in the dark. She found herself looking around, as if she had never been here before—as if she didn't recognise any of it. Was it really here that she had given her virginity to this man and stupidly reactivated all those deeply buried feelings for him?

'Come outside and sit down,' said Theo, still with that cool and remote manner which was making him seem like a stranger.

'I'd better go and pack,' she said stiffly, her fingers curling round her black patent clutch bag.

He frowned. 'You don't need to do that now, do you?'

'Well, actually, I do, if I'm leaving tomorrow.'

'This is news to me.'

'I wasn't aware that I had to run my travel arrangements past you first.'

'I'll need to arrange for my plane to be ready.' He studied her consideringly. 'Don't you want to stay for the reading of the will?'

A flicker of anger stirred to life inside her and in that moment Mia could have slammed her fists against his chest. Even the most insensitive person might have faked a little surprise at her abrupt departure, or fabricated a trace of disappointment, but not Theo. It was still about the money for him, she thought bitterly. 'I don't care about the damned will, Theo. I just want to get back.'

Something else which had been nagging at her suddenly occurred to her. 'What about Tycheros? Who's going to look after him now that Pappous has gone?'

'Don't worry. I'll make sure he goes to a good home.'

'A *good home*?' she echoed. 'With people we don't even know? Why can't you take him? There's plenty of space here for him to run around.'

'Because my lifestyle is incompatible with having a dog, Mia. I travel a lot of the time and wouldn't be here for him.' His mouth hardened.

'And I don't want the tie of having to look after an animal.'

Mia flinched at his words. He had all those staff but he didn't want a tie and he couldn't provide a home, not even for a dog as beloved as Tycheros.

'I want him to come to England to live with me,' she said suddenly. 'Will you help me do that?'

He loosened his black tie, his chiselled features sombre. 'So who's going to look after him while you're out all day studying? You need to think about whether that's what you really want.'

'Don't you dare patronise me!' She glared at him. 'I'll sort something out!'

His eyes had narrowed into jet-hard shards. 'You're looking very pale, Mia,' he said. 'This isn't a conversation we should be having now and you're not packing anything tonight. What you need is a drink.'

It was Theo taking control again. Theo being strong and masterful—and if she hadn't been so bone-tired, Mia might have challenged him. But the thought of going upstairs to remove her shabby suitcase from the luxurious wardrobe wasn't an enticing one, so she let him lead her out to the veranda.

The air was warm and thick with the scent of jasmine and the crystal glass into which he poured the brandy was as heavy as lead. She almost choked as the strong spirit burned its way down her throat, but at least the drink dissolved some of the tension which had been tightly coiled inside her all day. Or maybe it was just a sense of relief that her grandfather was at peace at last, which began to loosen some of her inhibitions.

This was her last night, she realised.

Her last night in Greece.

Her last night with Theo.

Tomorrow she would go back to her world, and he to his. She wondered how difficult it was going to be to forget him this time around. She wondered whether he would even give her a second thought.

Easing her feet out of her shoes, she glanced across the table at him. He had removed his black tie completely now, and although he had poured himself a glass of brandy, she noticed he hadn't touched any. His features were granite hard, his dark eyes unreadable. He looked so *unknowable*, she thought. And so remote. Just as he'd always been. As if what had happened between them hadn't made a dent in his iron-hard exterior. Had it?

'Before I go, can I ask you something, Theo?'

'What?'

Her voice was quiet. 'Have you cried yet?'

His eyes narrowed with a dangerous glitter, but his voice was deadly calm. 'Excuse me?'

'Don't do that haughty thing, Theo,' she said softly. 'After tomorrow, you'll never see me again so why can't we talk about it? My grandfather meant a lot to you and grief is supposed to be cathartic, isn't it? So…' She put her brandy down. 'Have you cried yet?' she persisted.

'Honestly?' He gave a short laugh. 'I have never cried.'

'What, *never*?'

'Never, ever, at least that I can remember.' The look he shot her was tinged with cold defiance. 'Satisfied?'

'Not in the least.' She studied him curiously. 'So, why not? Because you're a man and big men don't cry?'

He made an impatient sound with his tongue and for a moment she thought he was going to avoid the question, when suddenly he spoke.

'Because abandoned orphans have to fight to stay tough,' he informed her, his voice like gravel. 'And crying doesn't help you survive. Being rejected is bad enough but compound it with tears and you make yourself completely unlovable.'

It was the most candid admission he'd ever made and something about the raw and painful delivery of his words made Mia want to weep. But she didn't offer him the sympathy she suspected he would misinterpret as pity. Was *that* the reason why he didn't do love? she wondered. Because deep down he considered himself unlovable, even after all this time? Unwilling to give up, she tried a different tack. 'You're going to miss my grand-father,' she said.

He nodded, as if relieved by the sudden change of subject. 'I certainly won't miss his contrary nature or argumentativeness,' he said drily. 'But yes, I will miss the old rascal. He was...'

'What?' she prompted as he lapsed into silence.

'Nothing,' he said. 'It doesn't matter.'

She thought it did, but she let that one go. Her elbows on the table, Mia clasped her fingers together and rested her chin on them, her gaze very direct. 'Do you know the first thing he said to me, every time I went to visit him?'

'Since I've never been gifted with clairvoyancy, obviously I don't,' he drawled sarcastically. 'Is it relevant?'

'I think it is.' Her voice softened. 'Each time, without fail, he would look over my shoulder, and say, "Where's Theo?"'

'So?' he demanded brusquely. 'What of it? He probably wanted me to query something on his bank statement.'

'No, it wasn't that.' She drew in a deep breath. 'What I said the other day was true, Theo. You really were like a son to him—'

'Enough!' He sliced through her words like a guillotine. 'I am *not* going to sit here and listen to this sentimental hogwash.'

'Well, I think you *should*!' she returned. 'Unless, of course, you're too scared to hear what I've got to say.'

The silence which followed became so loaded with tension that Mia felt she could have reached out and cut it with a knife. His black eyes were blazing now—their dangerous warning unable to conceal the smoky flicker of lust. For a moment she thought he was going to come round to her side of the table, and pull her into his arms, and didn't her heart thump with painful longing as she found herself wishing he would? Wouldn't his angry kiss blot out all her pain and confusion—so that maybe she could reach out to him when he was soft and sated and more open to persuasion?

But he didn't.

His black gaze iced into her. 'Too scared?' he echoed furiously.

'What else am I supposed to think?' she demanded. 'You say you don't do family because you've never known one yourself. But that's not really true, is it, Theo? Because all that time, you had a relationship with Georgios which was better and deeper than many father-son relationships.'

'Enough, Mia,' he repeated warningly.

But Mia couldn't stop. She felt like a shaken bottle whose top had been wrenched off and all the words were spilling out—words she should have said to him a long time ago. 'You were more of a son to him than my own father was—you know that. He was proud of you, Theo. So very proud. Why else did he invest in your education and place so much hope in you? He relished all your achievements. Every one. And yes, sometimes he drove you mad with his cantankerous nature, but that wasn't enough to drive you away, was it? You were the one constant in his life,' she breathed. 'You say you don't do family, but he *was* your family. And you were his.'

'Mia—'

She thought he was about to berate her again but she was wrong. He was still shaking his head, but tears had begun to slide down his hard cheeks—rivulets of gold in the setting sun. He bent his head and buried his face in his hands, his big body convulsing with silent sobs. For a long time, Mia sat there, rooted to the spot, keeping a silent vigil over the weeping man she had never been able to stop loving. And when at last his shoulders had grown still, she pushed his untouched glass of brandy towards him and he lifted it up to quaff it back, in a single draught.

Still she said nothing, despite the bright glitter of his eyes which burned into her like black fire. She felt as if she were walking on a tightrope—one false move and it would all be over. Perhaps it already was. Because Theo was the personification of a proud, alpha man and she wasn't sure how this would sit with his image of himself. Would he resent her for bearing witness to his heartache and his pain? Would he regard his meltdown as an expression of acceptance, or weakness?

After a while, bright stars began to pepper the Saronikos sky and he seemed to stir himself, like a giant wakening from a long sleep.

'Are you okay?' she whispered, her words barely louder than the whirring call of the cicadas which surrounded them. 'Do you want to talk about it?'

A pulse worked steadily at Theo's temple as he thought about the candour of her question, and how impossible it was to answer with any degree of accuracy. He felt drained. Exhausted. As if he had just climbed to the top of a hill in the heat of the midday sun, the stones beneath his feet tearing his flesh to pieces. He was still trying to process some of the things she'd said, but although he had no trouble rationalising complex numbers, he didn't have the ability to do the same thing when it came to his feelings. He had no template for dealing with emotion. All he knew was that right now he felt empty.

In the starlight, only the oval of her face and the brightness of her hair were visible, her black funeral dress absorbed by the darkness. Her eyes were huge and her lips were soft, and a shuddered sigh left his lungs. She was a siren to his senses and, oh, how he wanted to take her in his arms and lose himself in her delicious heat. How easy it would be to alleviate the pain he felt with that.

He swallowed.

Easy, yes.

But simple?

No. Nothing was ever simple where Mia was concerned.

A pulse began to work at his temple. Just before her grandfather's death, she'd told him she wanted to go back to England, to carry on with her life, and she'd pretty much repeated that tonight. Why wouldn't she be eager to get away from a hastily conceived fake marriage which had served its purpose?

'I'm all done with talking,' he said flatly. He felt like a ghost, as if he had no real substance, and he rose to his feet and stared down into the upturned oval of her face. 'Would you mind very much if I called it a night? If you want dinner I can ask Dimitra—'

'It's all right, Theo. I'm perfectly capable of finding myself some hummus and pitta bread in the kitchen, if I get hungry.'

Her words were more than a little angry and more than a little hurt. As if he had disappointed her. As if she had been expecting something more. Some radical change of heart, perhaps? But Theo knew that this was the only thing he could do, for how could he promise something he might not be able to deliver, and disappoint her all over again? No. He must behave honourably and the best way to achieve that would be to sever his ties with her. For she was beautiful and kind, and he was damaged.

The scent of the jasmine which filled the air was beguiling his senses. He wanted to stay here. To whisper his fingertips over the silk tangle of her hair and then to bend his lips to hers. He wanted to stroke the soft satin of her skin and lose himself in it. But even as desire began to ripple through his body, Theo's hard-wired survival techniques kicked right back in. He needed to stay away from her and he should start the process immediately.

'I'll see you in the morning,' he said tonelessly.

Mia stood there mutely and watched him go, glad he wasn't witnessing the totally predictable tears which had sprung to the backs of her eyes.

Earlier, she'd thought she didn't have the appetite for packing but she had been wrong because Theo's cold words had tipped her right over the edge. She went upstairs and tugged out her battered old suitcase, careful to take only the clothes she had brought with her, staring balefully at the outfits and shoes which Theo had bought her. Let him keep his fancy clothes, she thought. She wasn't going to need them any more.

Her restless night was also predictable and she didn't see him in the morning either. But that was a deliberate move on her part. She waited until he had started his early morning swim before ringing for a taxi to take her to the airport, where she found a budget airline desk, because anything would be better than catching *his* plane. She might not be in megabucks Theo's class, but she certainly had enough money to buy herself an economy ticket back to London.

Afraid of her hasty departure being discovered by her husband, she didn't dare risk saying goodbye to Sofia and Dimitra, but she left them both an appreciative note of thanks. And although there were seven missed calls from him while she was waiting for her flight—before she finally took the courage to block his number—for Theo she left no note at all. Because what could she say?

I hate you.

I love you.

It was one of those strange things about human nature that both those things could be true at exactly the same time.

CHAPTER TWELVE

'YOU'RE TO GO up to the Presidential Suite right away, Mia.'

Mia stared at her line manager in dismay, wondering why she had gone to all the trouble of seeking her out in the staff canteen at this time of day, especially as she was officially off duty. Kirstie McLellan might be excellent at her job, but sometimes she forgot people were human. Or that they got hungry.

She glanced down at her toasted teacake. 'Erm, have I got time to eat this?'

'Not really. You'll have plenty of time for snacking later,' said Kirstie smoothly.

'But it's my—'

'There's a top-secret VIP guest expected within the hour,' Kirstie explained, seemingly unabashed by Mia's objections, or the rapidly cooling bun. 'And Mr Constantinides's office has just sent an urgent message down. Red carpet alert! We need to ensure that everything is as it should be, so I'd like you to give the entire suite the benefit of your expert eye.'

'Okay,' agreed Mia, trying to ignore the loud rumble of her stomach. It was ironic really, because she'd barely been able to eat a thing since she'd arrived back in England last week and had only just started to get her appetite back. All she wanted right now was to fill her face with some comfort food, in the wan hope that it might help alleviate some of the numbness which had refused to leave her, ever since she'd left Greece, and Theo. It was either that or going to her room to bury herself underneath the duvet and howl her heart out.

But she had her professional reputation to think of and the hotel had always been so kind and accommodating towards her, giving her the leave of absence she'd needed to visit her grandfather, which had been less than two weeks in the end. She could always add it to her overtime. And besides, nobody ever said no to Zac Constantinides, the big boss. With one last, longing look at her plate she took the staff lift to the top floor of the Granchester where, after checking the corridor outside for any dust or spillages—none found— Mia quietly let herself into the yawning expanse of the Presidential Suite.

The compact kitchen was gleaming, there was vintage champagne on ice and a mass of perfumed pink roses dazzled at the centre of the shiny dining table. So far, so good. It must be someone very important for the big boss to take a personal interest, she thought as she surveyed the pristine surface of the bed in the master bedroom and gave one of the velvet cushions an unnecessary tug.

She was just walking into the main reception room, with its famous view over London's Hyde Park, when Mia got the distinct sense that she wasn't alone. A sense which was confirmed when she saw the powerful body silhouetted against the huge windows.

She narrowed her eyes as a sharp arrow pierced her heart.

It couldn't be.

But it was.

Darkly beautiful and statue-still, Theo Aeton was standing and surveying her with an expression she couldn't work out—but what else was new?

How cruel life could be sometimes, she thought bitterly. Wasn't it enough that she was constantly haunted by him in her dreams? Surely she hadn't started to conjure him up in her daily life, too? She closed her eyes, but when she opened them again, he was still there. So he wasn't a hallucination at all, but real. Gloriously and vibrantly real.

The sharp arrow imbedded itself more deeply into her heart, penetrating through the terrible numbness which had descended on her like a grey cloud these past few days.

'No,' she said, her voice a reedy whisper, hating the instant prickle to her breasts as she looked at him.

He nodded, his hair gleaming like rich tar against the pale English light. 'Yes.'

She sought words to say. Something which wouldn't condemn her. She didn't want to tell him how much she missed him. Or beg him to hold her, or kiss her, or stroke his fingers through her curls, no matter how much she wanted him to do all those things, and more. She needed him to leave her alone to lick her wounds and recover, just as Tycheros had done in those early days when she'd found him.

'Go away,' she said huskily. 'Haven't we said everything that needs to be said?' But then she remembered how dismissive he had been with her on their last evening together and she screwed up her face into a belligerent scowl. 'And what are you even doing here, in my hotel?'

'I figured that booking out the suite was the most effective way of seeing you,' he said. 'Seeing as how you've blocked my number and won't answer any of my emails.'

'You could have always ambushed my room again!' she declared sarcastically. 'Don't tell me—you and Zac Constantinides are in some secret billionaires' club, where rich men are prepared to do each other *favours*, should the need arise?'

'Something like that.'

'That's outrageous,' she said automatically.

'I'm afraid that's how life works.'

'Your life, maybe. Not mine.' But she was feeling surprisingly calm, considering that her heart was banging like a drum beneath her pink polyester uniform. Had he told Zac she was his wife? She wondered frantically if that particular snippet of gossip would spread through the hotel like wildfire. Well, she wasn't going to be his wife for much longer, came her next grim thought. 'Is this about the divorce?'

'No, Mia. It's not about the divorce.'

'What, then? Hurry up, will you? I'm officially off duty and you're eating into my free time.'

Theo tensed as he met the flash of her blue eyes, which told him as clearly as her words just how angry she was. Had he thought she'd be so delighted to see him again that she would fling herself into his arms, without him having to redeem himself? That she would let him tumble her down on the bed and they could kiss and make up in the most delicious way possible?

Of course.

But nothing in life worth having ever came without a fight—he of all people should have known that. For the first time it occurred to him

that she really might not want him any more—
and could he blame her, were that to be the case?
He had pushed her away so many times. He had
erected barriers to stop her getting close and had
resisted all her efforts to knock them down. Yet
somehow she had managed to melt the icy cara-
pace which surrounded his heart, where every-
body else had failed.

He had underestimated her so many times and
in so many ways and, suddenly, he recognised that
this might be too little, too late.

Did he have a single chance left, or had he
blown it?

He thought of all the different words he could
use which might bring her round to his way of
thinking, though in his heart he knew there was
only one thing which might startle her enough to
listen to him. He could tell her that he missed her,
which was true, or he could use the words he'd
never said before. Was that what made his delivery uncharacteristically halting?

'Mia, I…'

She looked at him impatiently, her brows raised.

'I love you,' he said suddenly.

The sudden pallor of her face was the only in-
dication she'd registered the significance of his
statement, but her expression remained fierce and
defiant and he swallowed. She really was going to
make him fight for this.

'Is that why you pushed me away after my grandfather died?' she demanded. 'And why you acted so cold and remote? Is that the behaviour of a man in love? I don't think so. If you've come here because you want to have sex with me, then why not just come right out and say it? But please don't dress it up in pretty words you don't mean as a way of winning me over.'

Her taunt was provocative, but Theo stuck to all the things he knew he had to tell her. 'I have loved you for a very long time,' he said.

'Really? You've got a funny way of showing it.' But she screwed her face up suspiciously. 'How long?'

'Ever since I asked you to marry me, all those years ago.'

'No!' She shook her head and several coppery spirals broke free from her updo. 'Don't you *dare* lie to me—'

'These aren't lies, Mia,' he interjected softly. 'Why would I come all this way to lie to you? Of course I loved you. Why else would I have married you? Tying myself down with a wife at the age of twenty-three was the last thing on my agenda. I had everything I needed. I was on the road to financial success. I was able to have any woman I wanted and, no...' Anticipating another objection, he sighed. 'That wasn't intended to be an arrogant boast. I'm just trying to tell you the way it was. I didn't want anything more from your grandfather because he had already given me enough, but I most certainly wanted you. Hell, yes.' He paused, searching for something in her eyes, but they were still veiled and wary. 'I really, *really* wanted you. I'd never felt that way about a woman before.'

'Go on,' she said, though her tone was slightly softer now.

'I can see now that my determination to make us wait until we were married must have felt as though I were disempowering you. That I was guilty of taking away *your* choice.'

'Because you did. You treated me like a child, Theo.'

'Maybe I did. But you were only eighteen and I was very conscious of that.'

'That's no excuse. We didn't communicate properly,' she added fiercely. 'If you and Pappous had trusted me enough, you would have realised I would never have allowed my mother to take my inheritance away from me—especially not a piece of land which I loved so much.'

'Can you be so sure of that?' he questioned softly. 'She still had a big influence in your life. You believed her when she told you I was stealing from you.'

'I know.' She sighed. 'I should have stood up to her. In fact, I should have stood up to you all. But those days are long gone. It's all in the past now.'

She was biting her lip. 'And I still don't understand why you're here. What do you want, Theo?' she whispered. 'What do you actually *want*?'

He thought how speaking to a group of the world's most powerful financiers in a glitzy hotel in the south of France was a walk in the park compared to laying his feelings on the line to his wife. But what choice did he have, if he wanted to grasp the personal happiness which had eluded him all his life?

'You made me confront my grief about your grandfather,' he said unevenly. 'And to realise that, yes, he *was* my family. And once I had acknowledged that, I accepted it was but a small leap of faith to realise that I *could* make my own family work.' He paused, suddenly aware of the raw emotion in his words and his words were husky. 'But there's only one woman I want to have a family with and that woman is you. It's always been you. Nobody else but you.'

Still she said nothing. She really *was* making him fight. He drew in a shaky breath. 'I want to spend the rest of my life showing you how much I love you, Mia,' he said. 'I want you to forgive me for closing my heart to you, and to tell you that I will try hard never to do that again.'

'How hard?' she interjected suspiciously.

'Very hard.' He smiled. 'I want to have babies with you and make a family. A real family. And

I know your dream is to be a veterinary nurse, so I'm not sure how that would work, but maybe that's something we could look into. Now, I don't know if some or any of that appeals to you, but I need to hear your thoughts.' His throat constricted as he considered the possibility that she might refuse him and he wondered how he might bear it if she did. 'So, what do you say?'

What did she say?

Mia thought about it for a moment. Given their tumultuous history, wouldn't some women have held out for more? Hadn't she heard someone at work talking about making her man *grovel*? Well, maybe that was okay for some people, but not her. It smacked too much of manipulation and that was just not her thing. Because she had adored this man from the moment she'd met him and had never stopped adoring him, no matter how hard she'd tried. Her clever, charismatic, mercurial and always surprising Theo. The man who had been so short of real love despite all his stellar achievements.

She thought of the journey they'd travelled to get to this place and nobody could deny what a difficult and meandering path it had been—but none of life's paths were ever completely straightforward, were they?

What did she say?

There was really only one thing he needed

to hear. Eternal words which encompassed just about everything.

'I love you, Theo,' she said.

EPILOGUE

'YOU LOOK…'

'Tired?' Mia prompted as Theo's words trailed off.

'Different,' he said thoughtfully.

She finished removing her blouse and dropped it in the laundry basket before putting her arms around his neck. 'How?'

'I don't know.' His eyes narrowed. 'You look particularly beautiful this evening.'

'Theo, I don't.'

'Mia, you *do*.'

'How can I when I've been helping at the rescue centre all afternoon and the air-conditioning broke down?' She wriggled her shoulders and gave a satisfied sigh. 'And all I want to do now is to have a long, cool shower.'

'Mmm… What a good idea,' he murmured, unclipping her bra with consummate ease and bending his mouth to hook it around one rocky nipple. 'I just might join you.'

She giggled as they wriggled out of their clothes and turned on the powerful jets, her laughter quickly turning into gasps of pleasure as she wrapped her legs around Theo's back and he thrust inside her, the tiles deliciously cool against her back. Ecstatically her fingers dug into his wet flesh as he took up a hard and exquisite rhythm which made her gasp with pleasure. He knew her so well yet every time he made love to her, it felt as incredible as the first time. Soon she was shuddering out his name, revelling in his own urgent moan, which was drowned out by the gushing torrents of water.

Afterwards they dried off and wrapped themselves in light silk robes to wander out onto the bedroom terrace, where they sat on the swing seat in the soft heat of the early evening and gazed out at the gold-edged and glittering sea.

'Would you like something to drink?' he murmured against her damp curls.

But Mia leaned her head back against his arm and shook her head. 'Not yet,' she said drowsily. 'I just want to sit here and count my blessings.'

And there were so many.

Following Theo's declaration of love, Mia had left the Granchester hotel—the farewell party they threw for her was still being talked about weeks later—and had moved permanently to Greece, where she'd started learning the language in earnest.

After renewing their wedding vows in the same small church where they'd married the first time, Mia had laid her posy of pure white lily-of-the-valley on the grave of her beloved grandfather and said a silent prayer for him.

She had advised the veterinary nursing college that she'd have to let her place go—she was going to be busy enough learning Greek and setting up their new animal rescue centre. And being Theo's wife, of course. Because Theo *was* her life, as she was his. They enjoyed friends and concerts, eating out and reading. All the usual stuff. But her relationship with her husband underpinned her happiness.

A contented Tycheros now lived with them and Mia had been angling for a puppy to keep him company, and although Theo wasn't *quite* convinced, she was confident he'd come around to her way of thinking. He usually did. Her grandfather had left his entire estate to her, which she had ploughed into the rescue centre, where she volunteered as much as she could. Of course, that would all soon change because she wouldn't have quite so much time on her hands.

With the swing-seat rocking softly, she turned to look at the man beside her—at the dark chiselled profile which looked much softer these days—and her heart turned over with love and longing.

Sensing her gaze on him, he glanced down, his lazy smile indulgent. 'What?' he questioned.

'I love you,' she said.

'And...' His eyes narrowed perceptively. 'I sense there's an "and" coming.'

'I'm pregnant, Theo,' she whispered, her voice breaking a little. 'I'm having your baby.'

A split second of incredulity was followed by a look in his eyes which Mia couldn't properly describe, though later she tried her best, when they were lying in bed in the bright moonlight. She told him she had seen his hope and excitement—along with a tiny dash of natural fear. All the stuff which happened to every prospective parent.

As she gazed out at the metallic sea in front of them, Mia gave a sigh of blissful contentment...

Because most of all she had seen his love.

* * * * *

If *Innocent Maid for the Greek* swept you off your feet, then you're sure to love these other stories by Sharon Kendrick!

Secrets of Cinderella's Awakening
Confessions of His Christmas Housekeeper
Penniless and Pregnant in Paradise
Stolen Nights with the King
Her Christmas Baby Confession

Available now!

#4081 REUNITED BY THE GREEK'S BABY
by Annie West

When Theo was wrongfully imprisoned, ending his affair with Isla was vital for her safety. Proven innocent at last, he discovers she's pregnant! Nothing will stop Theo from claiming his child. But he must convince Isla that he wants her, too!

#4082 THE SECRET SHE MUST TELL THE SPANIARD
The Long-Lost Cortéz Brothers
by Clare Connelly

Alicia's ex, Graciano, makes a winning bid at a charity auction to whisk her away to his private island. She must gather the courage to admit the truth: after she was forced to abandon Graciano...she had his daughter!

#4083 THE BOSS'S STOLEN BRIDE
by Natalie Anderson

Darcie must marry to take custody of her orphaned goddaughter, but arriving at the registry office, she finds herself without her convenient groom. Until her boss, Elias, offers a solution: he'll wed his irreplaceable assistant—immediately!

#4084 WED FOR THEIR ROYAL HEIR
Three Ruthless Kings
by Jackie Ashenden

Facing the woman he shared one reckless night with, Galen experiences the same lightning bolt of desire. Then shame at discovering the terrible mistake that tore Solace from their son. There's only one acceptable option: claiming Solace at the royal altar!

HPCNMRA0123

#4085 A CONVENIENT RING TO CLAIM HER
Four Weddings and a Baby
by Dani Collins
Life has taught orphan Quinn to trust only herself. So while her secret fling with billionaire Micah was her first taste of passion, it wasn't supposed to last forever. Dare she agree to Micah's surprising new proposition?

#4086 THE HOUSEKEEPER'S INVITATION TO ITALY
by Cathy Williams
Housekeeper Sophie is honor bound to reveal to Alessio the shocking secrets that her boss, his father, has hidden from him. Still, Sophie didn't expect Alessio to make her the solution to his family's problems...by inviting her to Lake Garda as his pretend girlfriend!

#4087 THE PRINCE'S FORBIDDEN CINDERELLA
The Secret Twin Sisters
by Kim Lawrence
Widower Prince Marco is surprised to be brought to task by his daughter's new nanny, fiery Kate! And when their forbidden connection turns to intoxicating passion, Marco finds himself dangerously close to giving in to what he's always promised to never feel...

#4088 THE NIGHTS SHE SPENT WITH THE CEO
Cape Town Tycoons
by Joss Wood
With two sisters to care for, chauffeur Lex can't risk her job. Ignoring her ridiculous attraction to CEO Cole is essential. Until a snowstorm cuts them off from reality. And makes Lex dream beyond a few forbidden nights...

YOU CAN FIND MORE INFORMATION ON UPCOMING HARLEQUIN TITLES, FREE EXCERPTS AND MORE AT HARLEQUIN.COM.

HPCNMRB0123

HARLEQUIN
PLUS

Try the best multimedia subscription service for romance readers like you!

Read, Watch and Play.

Experience the easiest way to get the romance content you crave.

Start your **FREE TRIAL** at
www.harlequinplus.com/freetrial.